MURDER GOES GLAMPING

A PIPER HAYDN PIANO MYSTERY BOOK TWO

MALISSA CHAPIN

IVORY KEYS PRESS LLC

Cover design by BeckandDot Covers

Editing by Jonathan Wright

Sensitivity editing by Dr. Katherine Hayes

*To all my piano students—those who burped when they were nervous, those who worked hard,
those who didn't enjoy practicing, and especially to the student who gashed her knee
on her tiara—you've all enriched my life.*

"Beautiful music is the art of the prophets that can calm the
agitation of the soul; it is one of
the most magnificent and delightful presents God has given us."
—Martin Luther

PROLOGUE

None of this would have happened if Rosie hadn't made me go glamping.

CHAPTER 1

P iper Haydn's heart pounded and a wave of dizziness rolled over her approximately ten seconds after she waved off the Uber driver. She realized she had made a colossal mistake as his lights disappeared down Beach Road. Her hands twitched as she pointed her phone at the keypad on the door. Crickets chirped and waves lapped the shore, but Piper's fuzzy mind scrambled the code. She scrolled through texts, searching for the message from the cottage owner. She punched the correct code into the pad, and the door clicked open into a dark house. Piper slammed the door, twisted the deadbolt, and slid to the ground, choking back a sob. Tree branches scratched the window, and Piper jumped. Tears ran down her cheeks as she wadded a tissue in her hand. "This cannot be happening," she whispered. She stared at the bookshelves ahead, her eyes glazing.

The ticking clock grew louder every second, and the scratching branches plucked at Piper's taut nerves. She walked around the room, pulling the curtains tight and checking the deadbolt on the door, imagining sinister faces peeking through the bare kitchen windows. She sat on the white leather sofa, her feet planted firmly on the floor, and stared into the dark house.

Her heart raced as she tried to slow her breathing. She picked at the tissue and wiped her nose. Her head pounded, and her mind shouted questions Piper didn't want to answer. She would *not* let her mind dwell on why she sat alone in a dark Airbnb in Door County. She would figure out how to escape without getting entangled in the investigation because she wouldn't survive another one.

She swallowed a whimper. *Stop it, Piper. Calm down and think straight. Get out of here.*

The moon shone through the kitchen windows and lit a path across the rooms. Piper moved out of the light and stared into the darkness. Her mind ricocheted like a pinball in a pinball machine as she rubbed her arms, trying to focus. She walked to the desk in the entryway and picked up the welcome binder labeled "The Story of Beach Road Cottage." Piper ran her hand over the letters and settled into a chair near the curtained sliding glass doors. She tapped her phone light and pointed it at the words.

She counted her blessings that the cottage was open tonight. During the Door County tourist season finding a place to stay was notoriously difficult. With the Wisconsin Piano Teachers Conference, Glamper Fest at Peninsula State Park, and the Door County Lighthouse Festival, lodging was at a premium this week.

"I'll count my blessings and sit here hiding until I figure out what to do." She opened the binder and read:

> See what the Lord has done! I left a horrible situation four years ago. During bleak circumstances I drove and prayed. My tears were so thick I could barely see. I went to the land settled by my great-great-grandfather when he came from Sweden. As I walked through the snowy woods, I prayed and quoted Jeremiah 30:3—"I will cause them to return to the land that I gave to their fathers, and they shall possess it."

When we got an email from the property owner asking if we wanted to purchase my ancestral home, we jumped, and now we own my great-grandparents' house on Beach Road, next door to my parents. This is the house of my great-grandfather, where my dad picked raspberries with his grandpa, the house where I grew up next door to my cousins. During my destitute times, I prayed at the old homestead and believed that God would restore the land of my ancestors and heritage to me.

My children are the sixth generation growing up on Beach Road. God restored the land to me. This miracle property shows me he hears and knows. He loves and carries us, even when we don't understand why he lets certain things happen. He listened to my prayers. No matter what happens, he is still God.

Piper's heartbeat slowed as she read this stranger's story of God's provision. She wiped her tears and prayed. Maybe God would give her a miracle too. *Because I also don't understand why you let certain things happen. I hope you hear me like you heard this person. I'm pretty desperate right now. Please, God—help.*

She dropped the binder on the table and took a deep breath while remembering what forced her to hide alone and afraid in a stranger's Airbnb in Door County. "If only I hadn't opened the letter," she whispered. "Maybe everything would have turned out all right." Piper leaned her head back on the cushioned chair and closed her eyes, hoping to dream of anything other than the things crushing her heart.

CHAPTER 2

Two weeks earlier

Piper Haydn groaned and dropped the tool she held. She reached toward the ceiling to stretch. "Rosie, I cannot believe you convinced me to do this. I wanted to hire someone."

Rosie laughed. "Come on. A little physical labor is good for the soul. We're making progress."

Piper glanced around the room. Wallpaper hung in strips from the walls, and shreds littered the tarp on the floor below. Piper's arms ached from reaching above her head to steam wallpaper off the wall in the turret room of her old Victorian mansion. Her fingers stuck together from ancient wallpaper adhesive and her back ached from perching on a ladder for hours on end. Piper's cheeks flushed from the heat and exertion. The cheerful sounds of Shostakovich's "Waltz No. 2" played from her app, but the music failed to perk up her exhausted mood.

Rosie perched on a ladder, scraping wallpaper with a smile stretched across her face, whistling while she worked.

"Aren't you hot and sweaty?" Piper asked.

Rosie dropped a strip of wallpaper. "Nope. I'm having fun—but I do hope that the plaster is solid underneath all this wallpaper." Her red curls peeked out from her blue bandana, and her cheeks blushed a healthy pink.

Piper stopped steaming the wallpaper and stared at her friend. "What did you say?"

"The plaster. Sometimes it's a mess under all these layers of wallpaper, but you never know until you get down to the bottom." Rosie smiled and tossed a chunk of wallpaper onto the tarp below. "You might have twenty layers of paper on these walls."

"Ugh. Are you suggesting we're never going to finish this project?"

Rosie waggled her eyebrows, and a huge grin spread across her face. "We'll never know if we don't steam all this wallpaper off."

Piper glanced at her furniture and piano in the middle of the room, covered in layers of tarps. She loved the turret room and wished she had never let Rosie talk her into doing this themselves. "How long will this renovation take, Rosie? I need my room back so I can relax. Right now it's stressing me out."

Rosie tucked a curl underneath the bandana wrapped around her hair. Her eyes lit up, and she smiled. "Who knows? Months?"

Piper groaned and climbed down the ladder. She plopped in the middle of the floor and rested her chin on her hand. "Rosie, it can't take that long. I have an academy to run; this room is my sanctuary."

"Well," Rosie said, "you're never going to get it done by sitting on the floor. Especially when you sit on the old paper." Rosie burst into laughter when Piper stood up with shreds of ancient sticky wallpaper hanging from her backside. Her giggle echoed around the room.

Piper rolled her head to stretch her neck. "I don't know about you, but I need a break. I'm going to Sweetberry's. I heard Dominique made a new recipe today. You coming?"

Rosie hurried down the ladder and unplugged her steamer. "Of course, friend. I never turn down an offer of Sweetberry's."

"I didn't say I was buying." Piper laughed and nudged her friend.

Rosie rolled her eyes and picked up her purse. "Let's go before I die of hunger."

Piper locked the heavy front door and reached into the cast iron mailbox on her porch rail. She pulled out a stack of envelopes and tossed the keys to Rosie. "You drive so I can read this pile on the way."

"Anything good in there?" Rosie asked as she parked the Mercedes in front of Sweetberry's.

"Nothing much—an invitation to speak at the Wisconsin Piano Teachers Conference."

"What?" Rosie shrieked. "What do you mean, 'nothing much'? That's huge."

"You know I'm not a speaker, Rosie, and my invitation is clearly an afterthought because the conference is two weeks away. Their first choice probably fell through." She tucked the mail into her Chanel bag and hopped out of the car, taking a deep breath. "Mmm. I smell the lake." The cloudless blue sky and sunshine teased Piper as if saying, *Come. Rest and relax.* Piper smiled. She wanted to read on the beach, but not today.

Rosie held open the door of Sweetberry's. "Come on, slowpoke. Something smells heavenly in here."

"Girls," Dominique Landry stepped from behind the counter, her long dark braids piled high on her head in a bun. "Where have you been? I've missed you." Her dimples deepened as she smiled. She stretched her toned brown arms out and enveloped Piper in a hug. She kissed Piper's cheek then blew a kiss to Rosie. "Sit. I'll bring you today's experiment." She pointed to a table near the kitchen and disappeared through the kitchen door.

Rosie sniffed the air. "Do I smell shrimp?"

Dominique hurried back into the quiet dining room. "Here you go, honey." She set muffins in front of Piper and a platter with two overstuffed sandwiches in front of Rosie. "Praline cinnamon muffins and shrimp po'boys. Eat up."

Piper laughed and patted her stomach. "I only stopped for a brownie."

Dominique waved her hand. "You can take one home. I need your opinion on these for the Cranberry Festival," she said and waited with her hands on her hips. "Don't worry. These aren't spicy."

Rosie chose a sandwich and chomped into the thick bread. Tomato juice dribbled down her chin, and her eyes widened. "Fantastic, Dominique." Then she dropped the sandwich and guzzled a glass of water.

Piper laughed and ate her muffin. "I'm sticking with the muffins. I don't trust Dominique and her opinion of what's mild or hot."

Dominique's deep chuckle rang out as she moved back into the kitchen when a timer rang. "You poor Wisconsin babies would never survive in Louisiana."

Rosie refilled her water and gulped down another glass. She wiped tears from her eyes and fanned her open mouth. "Phew! That's hot!" She finished the water and said, "Let me see the letter from the conference."

Piper slid the envelope across the table, and Rosie read out loud. "We'd like you to choose from the following options to present at our annual pianists and piano teachers conference: surprising practice tips, piano pedagogy, female composers." Rosie paused and rolled her eyes. "That sounds stuffy. Here's a good one for you, Piper: creating piano recital programs. You're good at that."

Piper shuddered. The muffin she had eaten rumbled in her stomach, and she grimaced.

"Oh, Piper. I'm sorry. I know the word *recital* drags up awful memories." Rosie wrinkled up her freckled face and pouted. "I wasn't thinking."

Piper tucked the letter into her bag. "Precisely why I'm going to say no. I'm not ready."

"Not ready for what?" Dominique asked.

"Piper's invited to speak at a piano teachers conference," Rosie said.

Dominque's eyebrows rose. "Girl."

Rosie smiled. "In Door County."

"Oh, that's it, my friend. You're going for the scenery if nothing else. But about the conference—Rosie's right. You're an excellent pianist and teacher, Piper. Maybe you should consider the invitation." She rested her hand on Piper's shoulder and squeezed. "How are you doing these days, honey? I've prayed for you every night. I can't imagine."

"Lots of therapy, Dominique. I'm surviving."

Dominique smiled, pulled a piece of wallpaper from Piper's hair, and handed it to her. "Well, ask your therapist about speaking at the conference. But you might want to wash your hair first." Her laughter spilled across the table and filled Piper's soul. Dominque's happiness warmed her like sunshine on a summer day.

"Thank you, Mrs. Landry. I will ask her. And this," she said, holding up the wallpaper, "is all Rosie's idea. We better get back to the mess."

Dominique chuckled and waved as the girls grabbed the muffins and hurried out the door.

Piper peeked back inside and said, "Definitely serve the muffins at Cranberry Festival, Dominique. They're delicious."

"Thank you, baby." Dominique smiled and blew Piper a kiss.

"Hear me out before you say no," Rosie said.

"No," Piper said.

"Come on, party pooper. I have a great idea, and I want you to listen." Rosie pouted.

"I've learned that whenever you have an idea, I get sucked into doing stuff I don't want to do."

Rosie giggled. "True, but this is a good one. Are you ready?"

Piper nodded.

"Glamper Fest."

"I don't understand."

"Glamper Fest. You know my van, Bess, is a glamper."

Piper raised an eyebrow. "That's what you tell me."

"Oh, hey—there's Officer Hunky. Wave." Rosie waved furiously, and Chief Maxwell lifted a finger from the steering wheel—a Midwest wave. "Why didn't you wave?" Rosie demanded.

"Because I didn't care to wave."

"You're secretly in love with him, aren't you? I can tell." Rosie fluttered her eyelashes. "So romantic."

"I am not secretly in love with Chief Maxwell. Knock it off. What were you saying about Bess?"

"Oh! Glamper Fest is at the same time as your piano teachers conference, and it's also in Door County. We should go together."

"I'm not going to either event, but you should take Bess to Glamper Fest. You'd enjoy that."

"Okay, you're not listening. Yes, you are attending the piano teachers conference because you're speaking, and I'm going to Glamper Fest. But you're going with me. We'll glamp at night, and you'll go to the conference by day."

Piper's eyes widened and she gasped. "Oh, no, Roosevelt Hale. I am absolutely never going glamping with you. Not in two weeks and not ever. You're delusional if you think I'd consider it for one second."

Rosie pouted. "Good thing I know you love me. Otherwise, I'd feel hurt by your adamant refusal. Hear me out."

"No."

"Listen." Rosie held out her hand and waved a finger at her friend. "You know, I sunk a lot of money into Bess. She's a new creation."

"Praise God!" Piper yelled. "My foot has never recovered from that moldy awning dropping on my toes." She grimaced.

Rosie laughed. "You are ridiculous. Bess apologizes. She never meant to hurt you, but she's all fancy now and ready to go glamping."

Piper raised her eyebrows.

"It's biblical," Rosie said.

"*What* is biblical?"

"Glamping."

Piper stared at Rosie. "Now you're being ridiculous."

"Seriously! The tabernacle. Haven't you read how God decorated his tent with gold and jewels? That sounds exactly like glamping to me."

Piper rolled her eyes. "Oh, my word, Roosevelt Hale."

"Close your eyes and picture this. Pine trees. Wind rustling through leaves. Bird calls and water. Stars at night and beautiful sunrises every morning."

"You left out the mosquitoes," Piper said.

"Think about it," Rosie said.

"No."

"Don't answer me right away."

"Nope."

"Sleep on it."

"Never."

Piper parked in front of Rosie's house.

"I'll call you tomorrow and see what you think." Rosie blew a kiss to Piper and hopped out of the car. "We'll get back to your wallpaper project too."

Piper waved and pulled away from the curb. "I am never going glamping with you, Rosie. Never." Piper laughed at her silly friend. "I don't camp—fancy or not. No, Roosevelt Hale, this is one battle you'll never win." She tapped the screen on the sound system, filling her car with the sounds of Tchaikovsky's "Swan Lake" to drive the horror of Rosie's camping suggestion from her mind.

The ringing phone woke Piper.

"Piper, what's this I hear about you going camping with Rosie?" Sarah Haydn's too-chipper morning voice blasted in Piper's ear.

Piper groaned. "How many cups of coffee have you drunk this morning, Mom?"

"Two. Now, what's this I hear about you camping? You can't be serious. Think of the bugs and the dirt."

"I already thought about that and told Rosie, 'No way.' Who told you I said yes?" Piper sat up and jammed her feet into her slippers. Sun streamed through the window and she glanced at the clock. Rosie said she would start steaming more of the old wallpaper at nine. Time to get the coffee brewing.

"Well, who *didn't* tell me is a better question. Becky at Kindred Spirits, Poppy, and Ruby told me. Maisy dropped the news on your father when he ordered his Earl Grey this morning."

"I imagine they're all laughing at me."

"They're taking bets," Sarah said.

"What?"

"Bets. They're betting on if you'll actually go and how long you'll last if you do."

"Are you kidding me? That's ridiculous. I can camp if I want to."

"Exactly," Sarah said. "We can, but we don't want to, right?"

Piper shuddered. The idea of days and nights in the woods surrounded by darkness and creepy crawlies didn't sound like a good time. "Right. Hopefully one of them wins the bet and gets rich." She laughed. "No worries, Mom. I won't break the Haydn streak of never camping. You need not worry about your only daughter."

"That's my girl," Sarah said. "I *do* worry. You can never be too careful. You never know what's going on out there in the woods."

"Exactly. I gotta go. Love you."

"Love you, sweetie. I'm glad I heard wrong."

"You and me both, Mom."

Piper brewed her morning coffee and stood in the doorway of her favorite room. The piles of old wallpaper on the floor and the strips hanging down the walls gave the turret an abandoned appearance. "Sorry, old room," she whispered. "We'll finish this project soon, and I can get back to relaxing here."

A knock at the front door interrupted her thoughts. "Come in, Rosie." The knock sounded again. She hurried to the door. "I said come in, Rosie. Oh."

Chief Maxwell stood on her porch, smiling. "Good morning, Miss Haydn."

Piper raised her eyebrows. "Chief Maxwell—what brings you here this morning?"

"I'm patrolling the neighborhood and making a few stops this morning."

"For donuts, I assume?"

"Oh, that's original, Miss Haydn. I expect better zingers from you." He grinned. "I thought I'd do a wellness check on you."

She gaped at the police chief. "A wellness check? What on earth for? Who called?"

He held up a hand. "Nothing like that. I'm concerned. I've heard some troubling news around town and wanted to ensure you aren't under duress."

Piper stood up straight with her hands on her hips. "What in the world are you talking about?"

"Well, Miss Haydn, word on the street is that you're going camping with Miss Hale, and I knew that wasn't right. I figured you were sending some sort of code and needed a wellness check. If someone is holding you hostage, blink once."

Piper stared at the man. *He has lost his mind.* Confusion swirled for a moment until she noticed the sparkle in his eyes. *He's making fun of me.* She took a deep breath, made herself as tall as possible, and pointed at the chief. "You, Chief Maxwell, are ridiculous. I understand. You think I'm too prissy and stuffy to go camping, but I assure you, I am not. I will do fine. Besides, it's not camping—it's *glamping.*" She sniffed and moved to close the door, but the officer doubled over laughing. "What?" she asked, glaring.

"Oh, Miss Haydn, I don't care what you call it. You won't last five minutes in the woods, but I wish you well."

"I *will* last five minutes, sir, and I'll last the entire time. I will have fun too. My glamping adventure is none of your business. Go save the world or something."

Rosie bopped up the stairs as Chief Maxwell was leaving. "Hey, chief."

"Good morning, Miss Hale. I'm off to save the world or something." His laughter echoed back to Piper, and she gritted her teeth.

"What was that all about?" Rosie asked Piper.

"Oh, Mr. Police Chief thinks I can't endure camping, and I told him I absolutely can, and he needed to go solve crimes and leave innocent people alone."

"So you *are* going glamping?" Rosie squealed. Her eyes sparkled, and she clapped her hands.

"Yes, I am, and I'm going to enjoy it too."

Rosie ran to hug Piper and rocked her back and forth. "I'm glad, friend. We're going to have so much fun."

Piper sniffed and rubbed her nose. "I don't know about fun, Rosie, but we must get this room in shape." Piper pulled up her music app and pressed *play* on the Rachmaninoff "Piano Concerto No. 2." Piano music filled the room.

Rosie grumbled. "Seriously? You're going to force me to listen to this?"

Piper smiled. "Yep. I'm deciding on a composer for the senior program, so you have to listen with me."

"Well, the problem is, I'm not listening—I'm enduring." She scrunched up her nose and swiped at a strip of wallpaper. "Who are your choices?"

"Tchaikovsky, Rachmaninoff, and Shostakovich," Piper said.

"Ah—the Russians." Rosie saluted.

"You're incorrigible, Roosevelt Hale."

"I am, and you love me exactly the way I am."

"It's true. Thanks for helping me with this wallpaper project."

"No problem. I'm glad you agreed to go glamping with me."

Piper held her tongue. Visions of bugs and too much nature filled her with fear. But that insufferable police chief wasn't going to have a reason to poke fun at her. She would go glamping with Rosie and she would enjoy it—or die trying.

CHAPTER 3

Thursday, or D-Day

T he sun rose over Piper's Victorian home, casting a warm glow
through her window. She rolled over and groaned. *D-day.
Why, oh, why did I ever agree to this?* She sat on the edge of
her bed, inhaling deeply to slow the anxiety swelling in her chest.
"Okay, I can do this," she said. "Only a few days. Piece of cake." She
dressed in jeans and a pink polo and wrapped a floral scarf around
her hair.

Piper brewed an extra-strong pot of coffee and slipped out to
sit on her porch swing while she waited for Rosie to arrive with
the implement of torture—aka her glamper, Bess. The birds sang
a cheerful song, and the sun cast a pleasant glow. A police cruiser
passed, and Piper gritted her teeth. If only Chief Will Maxwell
weren't so insufferable, she would never have agreed to go on this
expedition with Rosie. But she was stuck pretending excitement.
She would never let him or anyone else betting on her camping
abilities know anything other than the fact that she and Rosie spent
a wonderful time in her glamper. *Please let this be a great time.*

A van turned onto her street, and the horn blared. Piper stood with a groan and said, "Rosie's here. Time to face the music."

Rosie pulled her camper van into the driveway and jumped out. Her pink-and-orange muumuu billowed around her legs. She waved and called, "Beautiful day for a glamping trip, my friend!"

Her bright smile rivaled the sunshine, and Piper smiled back. She loved her quirky friend, and she would try her best to act like a good sport, but this trip seemed like the perfect example of a misadventure waiting to happen.

Piper drained her coffee mug and gave herself a pep talk. "I can do this. I can do hard things," she whispered.

Rosie ran onto the porch, her bracelets jingled, and her gold hoop earrings swung as she clapped her hands. "I'm so excited, Piper. You're my first glamping guest, and I wouldn't have it any other way. Where's your stuff?"

"Inside. Let me grab my bags and I'll help."

"Nope. You sit and drink your coffee. I pack everything in a certain order, and you'll get in my way." She ducked inside, collected Piper's bags, and scurried down the steps.

Piper waited on her swing as Rosie ran around her yellow van. When Rosie's smile appeared over the top of the van, Piper gasped. "What are you doing? Be careful."

"Tying your bags up here on top," Rosie said, grunting.

Piper rolled her eyes. "My bags better not fall off between here and Door County," she called.

"Nope. They're safe. I'm double-tying yours." She hopped down and walked around the front of the van. "I'll grab the last of your things and we can be on our way—after a stop at Ruby's for coffee, that is."

"Perfect." Piper locked the door and took an extra deep breath. She pasted on a smile and followed her friend down the stairs into the glamper, her heart beating a little faster and her mind searching for a way to escape at this late hour. But, of course, nothing rescued her. No last-minute mishap like rolling her ankle in a gopher hole or a gallbladder attack. *Shucks.*

She climbed into the van and widened her eyes. *I guess I'm doing this.*

Rosie started the van and patted the dashboard. "All right, Bess. Time to shine."

Rosie parked the glamper in front of Ruby's, and Piper hopped out. If she planned to get through this trip, she needed the largest coffee Ruby sold. The bell jingled over the door, and Ruby waved.

"Big day, Piper?" Ruby asked with a grin.

"Come on, Ruby. You too?"

"Well, I love you, my friend, but camping material you are not."

Rosie leaned over the counter and stage-whispered, "How much did you bet on her?"

Ruby laughed. "That information is top secret."

Piper rolled her eyes. "You all have no idea how sturdy the Haydn family is. I'm going to glamp and survive with flying colors." She tossed her hair and harrumphed.

Rosie winked at Ruby. "Get this one the largest coffee you have, and add a shot or two of espresso. I have a feeling that if I don't keep her caffeinated, she's gonna turn on me out there in the woods."

"Can't have that, now can we?" Ruby asked and chose a large cup for Piper's morning brew. "I'm proud of you, Piper. Trying new things is always a good idea. I'm sure you'll love it. Rosie did a great job sprucing up that decrepit camper."

"Indeed," Piper said and shuddered, remembering the ancient van the first time Rosie showed it off.

"Here ya go." Ruby slid a massive cup of coffee across the counter. "On the house today. Bon voyage."

Piper sipped the hot coffee and smiled. "You're the best, Ruby. Thank you."

Piper soaked up the Cranberry Harbor scenery as Rosie drove out of town. She waved at everyone they passed.

"What are you doing?" Rosie asked.

Piper pouted and said, "Waving goodbye to civilization."

Rosie's laugh filled the van, and she cranked up the volume on the radio. "What am I going to do with you, friend?"

When they passed the Haydn orchards, Piper blew a kiss.

Rosie rolled her eyes. "We're not going to a funeral, you know, Piper. We're taking a little glamping trip in a delightful part of the state." Rosie narrowed her eyes. "What is Mr. Standerwick doing?"

"He's shaking the shovel at us. Good old Fergus." Piper waved, and the elderly man brandished his shovel again.

"What's his deal? I've never understood why he hates everybody. Why does he stay in Cranberry Harbor if he hates us?" Rosie asked.

"Who knows? My dad said that when Grandpa expanded the orchards in the '70s, they bought a corner of his property. He thinks Grandpa didn't pay him enough, and he's been angry ever since."

"At the whole town?"

"I don't know if he's ever been a cheerful person. I hear his son is an interesting character and a little kinder, but he's also old."

Rosie rolled her eyes. "Is he more interesting than our hunky police chief?"

"Rosie! Give it a rest!"

"I've seen him when you're around. The dude is definitely interested. If you weren't so formal when you talked to him, maybe he'd ask you out one of these days."

Piper turned in her seat. "I'm not interested in dating the police chief. We hardly know anything about him. Is he divorced? Widowed? Lived in his mother's basement until last year?"

Rosie laughed. "Well, he's a police chief, so he didn't live in his momma's basement until last year."

"Five years ago, then. I do *not* care, and I don't want you talking to me about him."

"Got it, boss. Roosevelt Hale has overstepped her boundaries and a certain Miss Haydn sends a warning shot." She saluted Piper. "Well, I'm not giving your love life any more of my brain power today. We have a road trip and glamping ahead of us. I'm so excited you came with me."

Piper smiled one of those "Dear God, please help me" smiles and nodded at Rosie.

"I know you're faking that smile over there," Rosie responded, "but I want you to know we will have the best time. I promise you."

Piper slouched in the passenger seat of Rosie's vintage VW van, holding on for dear life. Her legs melted into the sticky vinyl seat, and she bounced as they chugged along Highway 41. Piper glanced at the map app. "Are we there yet, Rosie?"

Rosie grinned, glancing in the rearview mirror before changing lanes. "Come on now—don't you whine like a little kid. This is fun. We're having fun. Let's play the alphabet game."

Piper pouted. "I can't believe I let you talk me into this, Roosevelt Hale."

Rosie's laugh filled the van, and she smiled. "I'm so glad I did. We're going to have the best time. I wouldn't want anyone else to be my first glamping guest."

Rosie switched the radio to a country station and sang her heart out to a song about a lost pup. Her hoop earrings jingled while she belted out the lyrics, and a pink blush rose on her cheeks to match the pink-and-orange floral muumuu she wore.

Piper loved Rosie dearly, but this trip stretched the limits of their friendship. She didn't understand exactly when she had agreed to go glamping with Rosie, but here she was on the highway to Door County in Rosie's vintage camper van—refurbished as a glamper.

"Come on—admit it. Kennedy and I did a good job on this project," Rosie said.

Piper glanced around the space behind the passenger seat. A sparkling chandelier hung over the tiny hand-painted table perched in the middle of the van. Rosie had reupholstered the dual-purpose bench seats in cheery yellow vinyl with white piping. On the opposite side of the van stood a tiny counter, a camper-sized fridge, and a sink almost large enough to hold two plates. Rosie had sewn curtains from a piece of vintage mod-floral fabric. The bright blue-and-yellow curtains hung over privacy shades, and a blue-and-white crocheted throw spread across the bench added a cozy touch. Rosie's brothers Truman and Harrison had laid down new black-and-white checkered flooring, and her brother Lincoln had painted the van and refinished the chrome at his auto body shop. The gear and their luggage rode on top, piled high and tied down to the metal rack at the front of the van. Piper hadn't watched Rosie pack everything on top. Instead, she sat on her porch swing chewing her fingernails and resisting the urge to throw up.

"You and your presidential siblings worked a miracle here," Piper said, wrinkling her nose, remembering the moldy fabric and stale air that assaulted her senses the first time Rosie showed off the van. "But you should have invited them to come along on your inaugural trip."

Rosie bopped to the music. "Nope. There's not enough room in here for my big old family. Besides, the date of the glamping fest matched perfectly with your piano teachers conference." She reached over and patted Piper's leg. "How lucky, right?"

Piper smiled, but her scalp prickled. The Haydns' idea of roughing it meant staying in fine hotels and eating at dining establishments with a permanent chef. Piper didn't remember the last time her family had lit a fire in their patio fireplace, much less a time when they cooked over the fire or slept outside.

Piper bit her lip. *What's bothering me?* She ran through her list of items but distinctly remembered packing each one. She played with the ends of the pink floral scarf tied around her hair and shrieked, "Rosie! Where's the toilet?"

"You need me to pull over? I told you that large coffee from Ruby's would cause trouble."

"No," Piper said, her throat dry. "Where's the toilet in this glamper?"

Rosie laughed and wiped her eyes. She slapped the steering wheel. "Piper, you're hilarious. There's no toilet in here. Not enough room."

Piper rubbed her temples. "Roosevelt Hale, you lured me on this trip under false pretenses."

"I did no such thing, Miss Posh. You've seen the inside of this van a hundred times. Where did you think the toilet was?"

Piper rested her head on the window and groaned. "I don't know, Rosie. I assumed."

Rosie's laugh filled the van, and her eyes sparkled. "You'll have to use the public restroom at the park like all the rest of us peasants, Miss Haydn."

Piper shuddered and her stomach lurched. *Oh, dear Lord—what have I gotten myself into?*

Rosie chatted a mile a minute, and her animated voice filled the van. Rosie's mouth moved, but Piper didn't hear a word. Her mind attempted to balance the lack of a bathroom with Rosie's excitement. She didn't want to hurt her friend, but really? No toilet? Piper closed her eyes, dreading the long days ahead full of bugs and public restrooms.

"Did I miss our exit?" Rosie said.

Piper's eyes popped open, and she checked the app. "Yes, you just missed Highway 57."

"I'll do a U-ey." Rosie turned into the open spot in the median and pulled back onto the highway, going in the other direction.

"That's illegal, you know."

Rosie giggled. "Yeah, who's gonna pull me over up here? Officer Hunky is nowhere around."

"Roosevelt!" Piper warned.

"What? He *is* hunky, and I saw him talking to you after church last week. What was *that* about?"

"He said hello and inquired after my well-being."

"Mmm-hmmm."

"Stop it."

Rosie smiled and sang along with the radio. Piper bit her tongue. She despised country music, but Rosie loved the stuff, and this *was* her van.

"Don't you want to listen to the Shostakovich playlist I made last night?"

Rosie chuckled. "Not when I can listen to Tangled Lines." She leaned over and cranked the radio. Bagpipe wails blasted through the speakers.

Piper's jaw dropped, and she rubbed her temples. "Oh, no. Bagpipes? Are you trying to kill me?"

Rosie giggled. "That's how 'Back Home Again' starts, but hang in there. I love this one." She sang along with the radio, "Back home with yooooooou," while Piper stared at her, speechless.

"What composer did you choose for the spring recital?" Rosie asked when the song ended.

Piper shuddered. "Let's call the program something other than *recital*—too many terrible memories. But I'm wavering between

Shostakovich and Rachmaninoff. I need to decide while I'm at the conference so I can order music for the students on time."

"What else do you have to do besides teaching three workshops, attending a million others, and picking your composer for the senior students?"

"Dad wants me to stop at the orchard stores in Door County to see if we're missing any merchandising ideas."

Rosie rubbed her tummy and licked her lips. "I'll go with you for that job, for sure. That big orchard on Highway 42 gives free samples."

Piper laughed. "That's true, but you know you can get samples and freebies at *our* orchard store, right? When we get home, stop in and try his new recipe—barbecue cherry potato chips."

"Oh, I will, but what if this orchard has better food?" Rosie snickered.

"You're lucky you're driving, or I'd throw something at you," Piper said.

Rosie stuck out her tongue and turned off the highway at the correct exit. "We're on our way, we're on our way, on our way to Door County," she sang at the top of her lungs.

Piper joined in, and they sang the new lyrics to an old children's song for several miles. Piper relaxed as the van rolled along. The scenery changed, and a familiar excitement filled her heart. The Haydn family enjoyed many relaxing getaways to Door County, and Piper had spent many idyllic summer days here. The beautiful scenery, charming towns, and quiet pace drew tourists from all over the United States.

"Kinda funny that we're escaping our tourist town for another tourist destination," Rosie said.

"Well, it's a different type of tourist destination. It feels like a pleasant break."

"Do you need a quick stop at any of the chain stores before we pass Sturgeon Bay?"

"I think I can survive a few days without chain stores."

Rosie smiled. "The park ranger said check-in is at three. We'll get to the park right on time. We'll set up and roast weenies over the campfire tonight."

Piper plastered on her fake smile. "Oh, great."

Rosie turned into the entrance of Peninsula State Park at exactly 3 p.m. The temperature cooled as Rosie drove along the tree-lined road, and Piper rolled down the van window to inhale fresh air and the scent of pine trees. She smiled at the sound of wind rustling through the leaves.

Rosie parked in their assigned camping space and clapped her hands. "You're gonna love glamping, Piper. I'm positive."

"I'll enjoy the fresh air and time with my friend, but we'll see about the glamping." She hopped out of the van and sank into a puddle. She lifted her foot and gritted her teeth. "I will not survive," she whispered as she bent to retrieve her ballet flat from the mud. Rosie scurried to the van's top and tossed bags and boxes. "Look out below!" she hollered, and a box landed with a thud next to Piper.

Piper covered her head with her hands. "Good grief, Rosie—watch where you're throwing things. There's a puddle here."

A golf cart zipped into their campsite, and a park ranger marched toward Piper. He pointed his finger and waved at the piles. "Campers may not leave their campsite in this condition. Clean up these piles."

Rosie hopped down and leaned two blue-and-white vintage lawn chairs against the van. "That's my fault. We're setting up. I'll have it cleaned in a jiffy." She smiled and reached to shake the ranger's hand, but he turned away and started the golf cart.

"I didn't get your name!" Rosie called.

"Roberts," he growled and pulled onto the road and disappeared.

"Grouch!" Rosie yelled.

"Shh," Piper said. "You'll get us in trouble."

Rosie laughed. "He doesn't scare me. All right, give me a hand here."

An hour later Piper and Rosie pulled the yellow-and-white striped canvas awning out from the van and arranged a table and lawn chairs around a blue floral outdoor rug. Rosie strung lights from the trees around the organized site and lit a campfire.

Rosie stood with her hands on her hips. "Well, Piper, what do you think? Come on. Rather charming, right?"

Piper glanced around and nodded. "I'll agree it's pretty. Now, where is the bathroom? I need to rinse this dried mud off my shoe."

Rosie opened the park map and pointed out the facility several spots up the road.

Piper groaned. "I cannot believe I let you talk me into this, Roosevelt Hale." Piper hurried down the road, the sound of Rosie's laughter following.

Piper hiked back to the campsite, grumbling. Her wet shoe squeaked, but at least her foot was clean. "I will not survive days of glamping," she muttered, but she pasted on a smile and waved at Rosie.

Rosie smiled when Piper sat in a lawn chair near the fire. "I love this. All of this." She waved her hand around the campsite. "I'm so happy you're the first person who came with me." She patted Piper's arm.

Piper jumped up. "My ride to the meet and greet will arrive soon. Are you sure you're safe out here all alone?"

"Of course," Rosie said. "Glamper Fest kicks off tonight, and I have a Glamper Fest get-together." Rosie pointed to the vintage camper driving past their site. "See?"

Piper closed the curtains inside the van and changed from her comfy traveling clothes into a navy blue pencil skirt and a coral blouse. She tied a navy blue and white checked scarf into a fancy knot and ran a brush through her hair. A touch of gloss, and she was ready to go.

"Well, Miss Piper, the piano teacher is back," Rosie said when Piper stepped out of the van.

Piper rolled her eyes.

Rosie pointed to Piper's conservative outfit. "You need some excitement, friend."

"Believe me, Rosie, camping with you is excitement enough."

"Glamping," Rosie said. "Glamping is glamour camping. Get it right."

The ranger on the golf cart zipped into their space. "Ladies, you claimed the campsite ten minutes before your reserved time." He peeled a piece of paper from his pad and handed Rosie a ticket.

Rosie jumped from her lawn chair. "Now, you wait a minute," she yelled. Her eyes blazed as she pointed at the park ranger.

Roberts sat down in the cart. "Press your luck, little lady. I'll kick you out of the park for disturbing the peace."

Rosie gasped. "You can't do that."

Roberts' eyebrows raised. "Watch me," he said.

"Fine. Write me as many tickets as you wish. I'm wallpapering my glamper with all of them." Rosie raised her chin and stared at the ranger.

His face turned red, and he pointed at Rosie. "It's a camper, not a glamper. *You* are the glamper. The vehicle is a camper."

Rosie waved her hands in the air. "I'll call my glamper whatever I want, and that is none of your concern. Glamper.

Glamper. Glamper." She shouted, getting louder with each word. "Furthermore, this isn't a campsite. It's a glampsite."

Piper patted Rosie's arm. "Let it go, Rosie."

"You better get your red-haired friend under control. I won't tolerate any disturbances in this park." He jumped in his golf cart and sped away.

"What in the world?" Rosie turned to Piper. "What did we do to him?"

"Who knows, but we should use caution. Sounds like he wants an excuse to kick us out of the park."

Rosie stood with her hands on her hips and stared down the road, muttering under her breath.

"You should karate chop him next time," Piper laughed.

"Not funny," Rosie said. "You know I don't actually know karate."

A car stopped at their site, and Piper waved to Rosie. "See you tonight!" she called.

Piper stood in the hallway of the convention center. Piano music played softly in the background. She listened for a moment. *Chopin? Yes—a nocturne*. Piper glanced at her watch. The teachers from her academy should arrive at any moment. They planned to meet in the entryway at seven. She took a glass of water and an hors d'oeuvre while she waited. *Mmm. Artichoke and puff pastry—my favorite*. The hall filled with the buzz of excited piano teachers as she walked toward the grand piano in a corner. A tuxedo-clad man sat on the bench playing the Chopin piece.

She stepped away to avoid disturbing his concentration and bumped into a woman. "Oh, my goodness. I'm sorry." Piper found a napkin and bent down to dab the water she had spilled on the carpet. Piper focused on the woman's five-inch-high stilettos and tight red leather pants. She grimaced. *Those heels hurt* my *feet.* Piper dabbed the spill and stood. The woman wore her hair piled high in a 1960s beehive-type hairdo and bright red chunky eyeglasses. Her bright red lipstick clashed with the orange floral blouse she wore.

"I'm so sorry," Piper said. "I didn't see you when I turned around."

The woman smiled and waved a hand. "No worries, doll. I wasn't paying attention either. I'm so clumsy." Her eyes widened and she pointed at Piper's name tag. "Piper? Piper Haydn? Oh, my goodness. I haven't seen you since . . . what? Sixth grade?"

Piper stared blankly, searching her mind for a memory of meeting this woman. *Surely I'd remember a girl like this. Wouldn't I?*

"Carolyn." The woman said, pointing to her name tag.

Piper nodded but didn't recall meeting this woman who did not dress like a piano teacher. "I'm so sorry, but I don't remember your last name."

"Sharpe!" the woman squealed. "C#. You don't remember me?"

"Ah. Carolyn—I'm sorry. How long has it been?" Piper said as memories of C#, as she called herself, flooded Piper's mind.

A shrill laugh erupted from the woman. "Oh, I'd say twenty years, Piper. So you still play?"

Piper smiled and nodded. "Of course. You too?"

Carolyn smiled. "And teach, but of course, that's why we're all here."

Piper forced a smile and nodded. "Where did your family move when they left Cranberry Harbor, Carolyn?" Piper hadn't kept track of Carolyn when they left. Instead, she and Rosie went to Sweetberry's and bought plates full of Mrs. Landry's beignets to celebrate. Carolyn single-handedly ruined every day of Piper's fourth, fifth, and sixth-grade years. She retained only ugly memories of C# and hadn't thought of her in ages.

Carolyn cackled. "Where *didn't* we move? Eau Claire, Rhinelander, La Crosse, and even Madison. You name the town, and the Sharpes lived there." Her laugh blasted out again, and Piper grimaced.

"What did your father do?"

Carolyn waved her hand. "Oh, you know—a little of everything. Well, I better catch up with my friends. Nice seeing you, Piper." Carolyn turned away and whirled back, her hands on her hips and her eyes narrowed. "How many students do you teach?"

Piper had completed the academy roster that morning, right before Rosie pulled up to whisk her away in the glamper. "My academy has five hundred and sixty-three students as of this morning." She smiled.

Carolyn's eyes hardened, and she curled her lips. "You always wanted to be better than everyone else, didn't you? My goodness, Miss Hoity Toity."

Carolyn wobbled away on her stilettos, and Piper blew out a breath. *Miss Hoity Toity, huh? Well, I'm camping. So there.*

Carolyn always had a weird obsession with beating Piper. School was the worst, but when Carolyn competed against Piper at the state piano championships, she skewered Piper with barbs and zingers. Carolyn picked off Piper's friends with lies and rumors and ruined the fun of piano competitions with underhanded tricks and harsh comments.

Piper remembered when Carolyn spilled soda across Piper's piano solo music. And the time Carolyn left the piano bench too close to the edge of the stage. Piper tripped and face-planted while dragging the seat back to the piano. The judges and students gasped, but Piper lay on the floor and prayed—specifically that God would open the earth and swallow her whole because walking to the piano and playing her piece gracefully were now impossible. She survived and occasionally used that story to teach her students how important it was to keep playing after making mistakes. She would say, "If I can play after face-planting on stage at a competition, you can keep playing after you make a mistake."

What were the odds of running into my childhood nemesis at the piano teachers conference?

When Piper returned to the campsite, Rosie was sitting and staring into the fire. "Have a good time?" she asked.

Piper sank into the lawn chair next to her friend. "Oof."

"That bad? You enjoy that piano teacher stuff," Rosie said.

"You'll never guess who I ran into at the meet-and-greet."

Rosie tapped her lips with her index finger. "Hmmm . . . I don't know. Did all of our teachers show up?"

Piper nodded.

"Let me guess—C#."

Piper turned to stare at Rosie. "Why did you guess Carolyn?"

"I have my ways," Rosie said, laughing. "But the third time Mr. Park Ranger stopped to yell at me, he asked where I lived. When I said Cranberry Harbor, he said, 'Cranberry Harbor? My wife grew up in Cranberry Harbor.' We had quite the conversation, and he said she's a piano teacher in Egg Harbor."

"Well, if the park ranger was that grouchy before he discovered we knew Carolyn, I can't imagine how he'll treat us now."

"Right? So how is she as a grown-up?"

"All I can say is 'Oh, my.'"

Rosie laughed. "She was always a bit of a mess, wasn't she?"

Piper nodded. "I haven't thought about her in years. She told me her family moved all over the state. Maybe she never fit in anywhere."

"So she terrorized poor, innocent children?" Rosie said, shaking her head. "That's ridiculous."

"She was a kid herself, Rosie. My mom always said to pray for her when she mistreated me, and I hated that. I wanted to treat her the same way she treated me." Piper laughed.

"Your mom's right," Rosie said. "I'll pray for her to have an anvil dropped on her head."

Piper laughed and patted Rosie's arm. "Everyone needs a Rosie in their life. I need to get some sleep. What are you doing all day tomorrow while I'm at the conference?"

"Being lazy and touring everyone else's glampers with a few of the people I met. We plan to drive into town to eat at the Swedish restaurant with goats on the grass roof and check out a museum or two."

Piper gave her friend a thumbs-up and stood to stretch. "Sounds wonderful. See you in the morning." She went into the glamper and changed. She closed her eyes before she had time to think about sleeping in the woods in an old van surrounded by dirt and bugs and who-knew-what-else. She squeezed her eyes shut and prayed she would dream of the Ritz and room service.

CHAPTER 4

Friday

T he sun peeked between the curtains, and Piper glanced
around. Loud snoring from Rosie's bunk in the pop-up roof
filled the van. Piper rubbed her eyes and rolled off the sleeping
bench—*can't call that thing a bed*—threw on a sweatshirt and
tiptoed out of the camper for the morning trek to the public
bathroom. She strolled past several vintage campers, smiling at each
site's cheerful touches and colorful decorations.

A soft mist rose over the ground, and when the sun shone over
the treetops, Piper's grumpiness dissipated. *Maybe glamping isn't
all bad. What a view!* A couple walked past her carrying kayaks.
"Where are you kayaking?" she asked.

"Straight ahead. Over that hill is the perfect spot." The man
pointed down the trail and waved.

*Maybe I'll have time to kayak the last morning before we head
home.*

The late-August air carried a bit of a chill, and she inhaled,
detecting a hint of autumn.

Piper moseyed back to the glamper enjoying the trees and the morning quietness in the park. The day ahead held seminars and meetings, and she would present the award for the piano teacher of the year later that evening.

The ranger pulled his golf cart next to her on the path. He parked and leaned out. "Wild party at your site last night. Did your crazy little friend tell you she screamed at me?" His hard eyes stared, and a chill ran up Piper's spine.

"No, I didn't hear anything about screaming, Mr. Roberts."

"*Ranger* Roberts to you. Well, you better corral your disastrous friend. I have my eyes on you two, and you're about to get kicked out of the park. We don't allow unruly campers here."

Piper lifted her chin and stared at him. "If you'll excuse me, Ranger, you are mistaken. My friend and I are not troublemakers, and we intend to obey the rules."

The ranger clenched his fist. "I know who you are and what you've done. All I'm saying is—Watch your step."

He sped off, leaving Piper staring down the road at his disappearing cart. "What have I done?" she yelled at the retreating park ranger, but he disappeared down the road.

She hurried back to Rosie's glamper, waving at people as she passed. When she returned to the camper, she climbed up to the pop-up roof and jostled Rosie awake. "Rosie, what's this about you screaming at the ranger?"

Rosie groaned and stared at Piper with red-rimmed eyes. With her hair tied up in pink curlers and a chiffon scarf, she was the perfect picture of a 1950s housewife—not a trouble-making modern-day camper. "What are you talking about?" she mumbled.

"Mr. Park Ranger warned he will kick us out of the park because of our infractions and you screaming at him."

Rosie rubbed her eyes and yawned. "When he brought the third ticket down, I might have yelled parts of Patrick Henry's speech as he drove off." She raised her eyebrows. "The man is ridiculous. I imagine C# filled his mind with a bunch of nonsense about us. Ignore him." She hopped out of bed and searched through the tiny cupboards in the kitchen area. "Coffee." She waved the percolator at Piper and tromped outside to light a fire and brew coffee. "Come out and join me. Drinking coffee fresh from the fire in the morning is amazing."

Piper settled into one of the lawn chairs while Rosie lit the fire. "Why does Carolyn hate me so much? I mean, we aren't children—why carry a grudge for so long? I don't understand."

"Some people love stirring up drama and keeping things going. Ignore her." Rosie poked at the fire and adjusted the pot on the rack over the fire. "Ten minutes to the best cup of coffee you've ever tasted."

"Better than Ruby's?" Piper teased.

"Well, the best cup you ever tasted *today*." Rosie's laugh filled the campsite, and Piper smiled. She loved her friend, and this morning outside the glamper the sun shone a pleasant glow on their campsite. But she preferred fewer bugs and pine needles in her living space.

"Ta-da!" Rosie yelled and handed Piper a mug of steaming coffee.

Piper took a sip, and her eyes widened. "Perfect—thanks. Oh, I won't be back in time for dinner tonight."

"That's fine. I have a busy day and I'm hosting dessert for the progressive supper at our site. Hope you don't mind."

"I don't mind. I'm glad you have activities to keep you busy while I'm gone. I feel less guilty for deserting you."

"Don't feel guilty for one minute. A day full of piano teacher gobbledygook sounds like torture to me. Besides, I can crank up my country music if you're gone all day." She giggled.

"Not too loud. The ranger seems ready to pounce," Piper said as her ride pulled up.

"I'll take care of that ranger!" Rosie yelled and waved her fist.

Piper hurried into the hall, greeted her teachers, and passed out the music-themed notebooks she had purchased at Kindred Spirits Bookstore before she and Rosie left Cranberry Harbor. She planned to sit with her teachers for the keynote speech—Professor Werth from UW Madison presenting "Pedagogy and Creativity." She asked them to take excellent notes of the various workshops—they would compare notes later.

The Haydn Music Academy instructors had settled into their row when a loud voice from the back of the room yelled, "I want to find Piper Haydn. Piper, where are you?" The woman screeched in a sing-song voice.

Piper's teachers turned to stare, but Piper slunk down in her seat and covered her eyes.

Carolyn wore turquoise leather pants, a lime-green gingham crop top with billowing puffed sleeves, and green stilettos. She marched to Piper's row, stood in the aisle with her hands on her hips, and nodded to the teachers. "Your boss here's been causing trouble for my husband out at Peninsula State Park. Tell 'em, Piper."

Piper jumped from her chair and spluttered. "Carolyn, you've got it all wrong."

"Are you calling my husband a liar?" A curl jiggled loose from Carolyn's beehive and hung down the side of her face. She scowled at Piper and turned to the teachers gathered around. "And my name is C#—don't call me Carolyn again, Piper." She marched to the front of the room and plopped into a chair.

"Sorry, ladies. I'll explain later." Her phone dinged, and she swooped it out of her purse to silence the ringer before the lecture began.

---Only one new ticket from Mr. Grumpy Ranger today. Ha.
---Be careful. I don't know what's going on. C# blasted me in front of everyone.
---Sorry.

Piper dropped the phone into her purse and glanced around the room. Everyone seemed busy with their groups. She settled into her seat as the lecture began, but her heart beat fast and her head ached.

Piper reviewed her note cards and waited nervously for the announcer to call her to the podium. She did not enjoy speaking, but she had agreed to teach one of the hour-long workshops. She planned to share tips for encouraging students to practice, and hopefully she would fill the block of time before she ran out of ideas to share. She would take questions from the room if she finished too early. Excited piano teachers chattered, and Piper's nervousness increased at the noise. She glanced around the room to find the exits. *Maybe I'll run before they call my name.* She rested her hands on her stomach, blew a breath, and whispered a quick prayer, *Lord, give me strength,* while she adjusted her music-print scarf.

The chair next to her jiggled. Piper turned to say hi, but her eyes widened when the face of C# appeared.

"You nervous, Piper? Don't be nervous. I'm right here watching you. Nothing at all to worry about." Carolyn chuckled. "I'll take notes on all of your mistakes."

"Carolyn, I don't understand why you despise me after all these years. We should let things go. Don't you think?"

C# stared at Piper. Her eyes blazed. "Piper, if you think for a moment that I'm over what you did to me, you're a worse human than I remembered."

"What I did to you? What did I—"

"Help me welcome Piper Haydn this afternoon." The announcer's voice cut into Piper's attempt at reconciling with Carolyn.

She jumped from her seat and passed Carolyn sitting in the front row, arms crossed. *It's going to be a long hour.*

Piper survived her workshop even though Carolyn often interrupted with loud harumphs and snorts. Her caustic comments and sarcastic questions tempted Piper to respond in kind, but she took a deep breath and kept talking. When the workshop finished and the teachers filed out, Piper blew out the breath she held and plopped onto a chair in the front row to gather her thoughts. She wracked her brain, trying to imagine what she had done for Carolyn to despise her so. Her husband had said, "I know what you've done."

"*What* have I done?" she whispered. The only memories she pulled from the recesses of her mind involved Carolyn terrorizing her. "I don't know," she whispered. She checked her messages—nothing from Rosie. Hopefully life had settled down at the campsite and they would enjoy their next few days in the park.

Listen to me saying "enjoy our days at the park." Ugh, Roosevelt. You're ruining me. She hurried to the next presentation, clutching her notebook and rolling her eyes.

"Piper, I enjoyed your workshop. Very helpful." A man dropped into the seat next to her. He held out his hand. "Scott Figsby. I teach piano in Stevens Point."

Piper clasped his hand and smiled. "Thank you." His blue eyes crinkled at the corners, and Piper caught herself staring at the handsome man. She glanced down at her notebook.

"Care to join me for dinner? I'd love to hear more about your methods. Your ideas inspire me."

Piper blushed. "Of course. I'm always happy to chat about teaching the piano." She smiled at the man and caught a hint of his cologne—something fresh, like the water in the bay outside the picture window.

"I'll find you at six in the restaurant if that suits you?"

"Certainly," Piper said.

He stood and smiled. "Six o'clock then."

Piper hummed a dreamy tune as he wove his way through the crowd. *Get a grip, Piper.*

The day at the conference passed quickly. Piper attended a session on women composers and another on hands-on activities to teach music theory. Several teachers talked to her throughout the day, sharing what they had learned and explaining their new ideas for the academy. Piper's head swam with ideas and inspiration.

Piper listened to her teachers sharing and discussing new ideas with pride. The Haydn Music Academy would benefit from this conference for years to come. She was glad she had paid their fees and invited her interested teachers to attend.

"Where's Rosie?" Betsy Farell, the new preschool music teacher, asked.

"Back at the park with her glamper buddies."

"Oh, that's right. She did such a great job fixing that mess of a van. You're so lucky to camp with her," Betsy gushed.

Piper smiled and stifled a grimace. "Lucky indeed."

A pianist played soft music in the background as Piper entered the hotel dining room. She waved to several acquaintances and searched for Scott Figsby. She crossed the restaurant to her group but paused when the waiter passed with a large tray. She startled at a touch on her elbow.

"There you are. I searched all over for you," a deep voice whispered.

"Oh, Mr. Figsby. Good evening." She breathed a sigh of relief that he had spotted her. She wanted to learn more about him and figure out why he interested her.

"Call me Scott," he said and guided her to an empty table for two along the side of the hotel dining room.

He held the chair for her as she sat. He smiled, and his eyes sparkled. "Are you excited about tonight? Professor Werth is quite the speaker. I'm sure both of us will learn something."

"Yes, between you and me, he's why I agreed to attend the conference. I can't wait to hear about his methods and ideas. I have my paper and pen ready to take notes. I hear he talks fast."

Scott laughed and Piper relaxed. The dinner hour passed in pleasant conversation and piano teacher talk. Scott told her about his student who belched at the piano whenever he was nervous, and Piper told him about the student who showed her an injury. "When I asked her what happened, she said, 'I fell on my tiara.'"

He laughed, and when he did, his eyes sparkled, and Piper laughed at his happiness. She pointed to the lake as a sailboat floated past, sails unfurled and an American flag waving from the mast.

"I love sailboats," she said.

He nodded. "Me too. And a sailboat in Door County? Even better."

"I love Door County. My family vacations here often."

"I try to get up here as often as possible, but it's never often enough," he said.

"Do you sail here?"

"I do," he said. "But getting through Death's Door is always challenging."

Piper shivered. "That's the passage between the mainland and Washington Island, right? Death's Door sounds so chilling." She rubbed her arms to tame the goosebumps rising on her skin.

He nodded. "When you think of the history, it certainly is chilling—over two hundred seventy-five shipwrecks. I never pass through the strait without thinking of the poor sailors."

She grimaced. "Enough about death for now—happier topic. How long have you played the piano?"

Scott shared with her his love of the piano. He had taken lessons since elementary school and studied piano at UW-Stout. Piper shared how she came to love the instrument, and the rest of the meal passed in light conversation. She tried to remember running into him at piano teacher functions in the past.

"Are you new to Wisconsin? Or new to the piano teacher guild?" Piper asked.

He leaned back in his seat and crossed his arms. "Why do you ask?"

"I haven't met you before, and I attend most of these functions," she said.

He smiled. "Well, I'm new to the guild then."

Piper frowned at his odd reply, but several of her teachers scooted past at that moment. "We'll save your seat, Piper!" Betsy called. Piper waved and excused herself. "Thank you. I enjoyed getting to know you this evening. Enjoy Professor Werth."

He nodded, and Piper hurried to catch up with her her teachers.

Piper scribbled notes furiously as Professor Werth spoke. She would never have time to implement all these ideas, but she wanted to gather notes on everything and discuss new ideas with her teachers later. Her mind buzzed with possibilities and plans as the professor's presentation continued. *This conference is what I needed to re-ignite the love of teaching after . . . well, after everything. I'm so glad we came.* She nodded and smiled as he worked his way through the outline. She glanced down the row at her teachers scribbling notes and smiled. Excitement bubbled in her heart. Last summer's tragedy was history. Her academy survived, and she survived—even thrived. After the conference she would go back to Cranberry Harbor brimming with new ideas for the Haydn Music Academy. They were moving onward and upward. Nothing but good. *Thank you, God. I needed this.*

Piper leaned back in her chair as the professor finished his presentation. She glanced up to copy a quote—"When words fail, music speaks. Hans Christian Andersen"—and watched as Scott

Figsby left the hall through the door to backstage. *That's odd. He said he came specifically to hear Professor Werth.* She scribbled the quote and focused on the speaker. Who cares if he left? She planned to get her money's worth out of this conference and would not leave early.

Movement near the backstage door caught her attention, but when she glanced up, she saw a flash of bright green. The person disappeared behind the door before Piper noticed who followed Scott, but that shade of green was the same color C# wore the last time Piper had seen her.

Piper moved to the front row to await the award ceremony. The conference organizer slipped into the spot behind her and leaned over the chairs. She handed Piper a thick envelope and whispered, "Read the script and open the small envelope inside for the name. Got it?"

Piper nodded and gave a thumbs-up as Professor Werth's speech ended. The hall erupted into loud applause, and the man's cheeks flushed. He smiled and gave a small wave as he hurried off the stage. The lights dimmed, and the organizer whispered, "Now."

Piper climbed the stairs and stepped into the bright lights on the stage. "Good evening, ladies and gentlemen. I'm honored to present the award for Wisconsin's outstanding piano teacher of the year." She eased the script from the large envelope and read, "This year's outstanding piano teacher lives and works in a small community. This teacher exemplifies the heart and soul of our association by tirelessly contributing to the musical life of local schools, organizations, churches, and individuals. For offering piano lessons to low-income children at no cost, the Wisconsin

Piano Teachers Association award for outstanding piano teacher of the year goes to . . ."

Piper smiled at the audience as she opened the small envelope. Her eyes widened and she sputtered, "Carolyn Sharpe." Applause filled the auditorium, and Piper forced a smile to her eyes. She didn't want to hear Carolyn Sharpe complain about the faces Piper made onstage during her proud moment. The petty childishness of years past bubbled up in Piper's heart, but she tamped the feelings down. *For heaven's sake, Piper. You haven't thought of Carolyn for years. You knew you weren't getting the award anyway, since you were the one presenting.* She smiled and glanced around the room as other attendees craned their necks, searching for Carolyn. Piper remembered the flash of green moving through the backstage door. If C# had left, why? Surely she must have known they nominated her for an award?

Piper smiled and said, "Carolyn Sharpe, you're Wisconsin's outstanding piano teacher of the year." Thunderous applause filled the auditorium, but no C#. The organizer ran onto the stage and picked up the plaque.

"Thank you, everyone, for coming. We'll see that Ms. Sharpe receives her award. Join us in the lounge for cherry sundaes." She reached forward, clicked off the microphone, and turned to Piper. "That's odd. I'm certain I saw her in this room during Professor Werth's presentation. Thank you, Piper." The woman took C#'s plaque and scurried to join the crowd below.

Piper scanned the room, but no sign of Carolyn. She left the stage to find her teachers—cherry sundaes sounded like the perfect way to end a long day.

"Hey, friend!" Rosie called when Piper returned to the campsite.

Piper smiled and waved. "Hey yourself. How was your day?" She settled into a lawn chair near Rosie and kicked off her shoes. The crackling fire and glowing lights around the camper bathed the campsite in a cozy glow.

"Busy. We toured each other's campers tonight and enjoyed a progressive supper. I got some ideas for making Bess cuter—if that's even possible. We caravanned to town, checked out some shops, and ordered lunch at the restaurant with goats on the roof."

"No way. You ate Swedish pancakes without me?"

"You bet I did—lingonberries too." She patted her stomach and grinned.

"And here I thought you were my friend," Piper teased.

"Hey—you know that when it comes to lingonberries, all's fair in love and war. Besides, I could eat there all the time. Let's stop there for dinner on our way out of town." She laughed and stood to poke the fire.

"What are you wearing?"

Rosie twirled around and kicked a leg out to the side. "Aren't they fabulous? You'll never guess where I found these!" The brown-and-orange plaid fabric pants billowed around Rosie's legs.

"Careful. Those are a fire hazard," Piper said. "Let me guess . . . a thrift store?"

"Yeah. A super-cool shop behind a hotel in Ephraim. *Gen-you-wine* 1970s bell bottoms with extra 'bell.' They have a paisley pair in your size if you want me to run back tomorrow."

Piper rolled her eyes. "As always, they are marvelous on *you*, Rosie, but you know I can't pull that off."

"Come on—live a little." Rosie nudged Piper and grinned. "Want a s'more? There's plenty left. I contributed dessert to the progressive supper—even though I hate chocolate." Rosie poked two marshmallows onto a stick and held them over the fire. She turned them around and lifted them in and out of the heat.

"I've never seen a person so dedicated to toasting marshmallows," Piper said.

Rosie rotated the stick. "Anything worth doing is worth doing well, my friend." She sandwiched the perfectly toasted sugary blob between two graham crackers and poked a square of chocolate in the middle. "Eat up."

Piper bit into the gooey treat and groaned. "Mmmm." She licked her lips. "Okay, if you perfectly toast marshmallows and feed me chocolate, I'll go glamping with you again."

Rosie pumped her fist in the air and danced around the campsite. "Yes! I told ya I'd win you over." She dropped into the lawn chair and waggled her eyebrows. "Victory."

"You're something else, Roosevelt Hale," Piper said, grinning.

Rosie bounced her red curls and grinned back. "And you love me exactly the way I am."

Piper winked. "You're right. What else did you do today?"

"We went to the museum. Oh, guess what—I found a mystery we can solve. Let me grab my notebook. Be right back." She rushed into the camper, her laughter echoing behind her.

Piper shivered as the flames danced. "I've experienced more than enough mystery for one lifetime. Thank you very much," she whispered.

The glamper door slammed, and Rosie dropped into the chair next to Piper. "You'll never guess who used to vacation in Door County!"

"No idea."

"Someone famous. I'll give you three guesses."

"Oh, man, Rosie. You know I'm not good at guessing games."

"Come on—try."

"Wonder Woman."

"Come on. Give me a real guess. You're a spoilsport."

Piper tapped a finger on her lips. "Hmmm . . . Donald Trump."

"Ha. Can you imagine? Nope. One more. Guess someone vintage."

"Zsa Zsa Gabor."

"Hey! That's an exceptional guess, but no." Rosie poked the fire and stared into the flames.

Piper cleared her throat. "Well, are you going to tell me?"

"Oh! Sorry. I got busy watching the flames. Wallis Simpson." She clapped her hands and grinned.

"Wallis who?"

"You know that woman that married the king, and he abdicated the throne for her?" Rosie fluttered her eyelashes. "So dreamy."

"I vaguely recall that from history. How did you learn this little tidbit?"

"The museum has a letter from her and a wedding invitation to a local girl. It's from her wedding to the first guy—not the king . . . cool though, right?"

"I guess. What's the mystery?"

Rosie opened the notebook and scribbled across the top of the page. "Well, it seems the museum owned an enormous diamond from the Duchess. Forty years ago it disappeared, and it's still missing. There's a reward too."

Piper laughed. "Well, if the people who have a monetary interest in it haven't discovered it in forty years, I don't think two girls from Cranberry Harbor will solve the mystery in the two days we have left in Door County."

Rosie smiled. "You never know. We worked together pretty well on the last mystery, my friend."

Piper shuddered. "Let's avoid bodies, okay?"

"Deal. I met some guy named Scott on the museum tour. He's here from New York for a few days. Tall, blonde, nice suit." Rosie waggled her eyebrows. "I got his number."

Piper's eyebrows raised. "Wow, Rosie. Picking up guys at the museum? Better be careful!"

Rosie laughed and poked the fire again.

"You know what's weird? I met a guy named Scott at the piano teachers conference, and we ate supper together. Tall, blonde, nice suit. But he's from Steven's Point."

Rosie's eyes narrowed. "What color suit?"

"Gray with a blue tie."

"Hmmm," Rosie said. "Sounds like Scott has a doppelgänger. I'm writing this down in the notebook."

"Either that or he's a weirdo," Piper laughed. "Guess who won the piano teacher of the year award?"

"You." Rosie guessed.

"No, and I won't keep you guessing. C#."

"What?" Rosie shrieked and jumped from her chair. She pointed at Piper and yelled, "How can someone still carrying a grudge and treating you ugly twenty years later be such an amazing piano teacher that she wins an award? She probably blackmailed someone on the committee."

Piper laughed. "Shh, before Mr. Ranger visits us. Who knows? Maybe there's more to C# than she lets on. They said she gives free lessons to poor students."

Rosie plopped into her chair. "Well, okay then. That's nice at least." She turned to the road and cupped her ear. "Good grief—here comes Mr. Ranger right now."

"How do you . . ."

A golf cart zipped into their space, cutting off Piper's question. The ranger popped out and marched to Rosie. "It's after quiet hours, and I heard yelling at this campsite. Noise violation." He handed the ticket to Rosie.

She jumped up and poked a finger in his face. "We know your wife doesn't like my friend, but that doesn't mean you need to find reasons to pester us."

His eyes narrowed, and he leaned forward and hissed. "I'm doing my job, and I don't appreciate your accusations, miss. One more violation and you two vagrants are out of my park." He marched back to the cart and turned the key. "And leave my wife out of it." He disappeared into the night.

Rosie sputtered and marched near the campfire. "What a jerk!" She huffed and whispered threats as she paced in front of the fire.

"Should we search for another campground to finish out the week?" Piper asked.

"Already did, but I'd miss all my glamping activities, and between the Glamper Fest and Lighthouse Festival, there's not a place to stay in the whole county. Can't even find anything available on the house rental site."

"Let's get some sleep. We'll figure something out tomorrow."

Rosie banked the fire and muttered. She turned to Piper with a scowl. "You know what's weird? That Scott guy I met reminds me of Mr. Grumpy Ranger."

"Really?" Piper wracked her mind to compare the Scott she had met to the ranger, but did they resemble each other? "Who knows, Rosie? I'm beat. Night."

"Night. I'll come to bed soon."

The crickets chirped, and a cool breeze blew through the trees, filling the glamper with the soothing scent of pine trees and leaves. Piper pulled the curtains and changed into sweats for the night. She yawned and stretched out on the bench-turned-into-a-bed and stared at the ceiling. *Rosie, I can't believe you talked me into glamping with you, but even though I'll never admit this to you, I'm enjoying the experience.* She yawned and rolled over, listening to the calming sounds of the nighttime forest.

Piper's eyes popped open, and she blinked while adjusting to the dark. *What woke me?* She lay on the bench and concentrated. Rosie snored softly in her bed in the pop-up roof, and the breeze rustled through the tree leaves above the glamper. A branch cracked. Piper's eyes widened as the pungent stench of cigarettes wafted into the camper. She held her breath and peered through the curtained window. No moving shadows. No frightening villains. Nothing. *Your imagination is in overdrive. Go back to sleep.*

She tossed and turned, her mind racing and fear rushing to the surface. She dozed fitfully, startling awake when her mind replayed the day her Steinway arrived—with the body of her ex-fiancé closed inside. She tugged the crocheted afghan around her shoulders and lay on her side, staring into the dark. She tapped her phone to check the time—three a.m.—a text from Dominique blinked on her screen.

---Praying for you to have a relaxing time, baby. Stop in when you're home.
I tweaked the beignet recipe.

Piper smiled. "If Dominique is praying for me, I should be able to sleep," she whispered and rolled over. She closed her eyes, but sleep eluded her. She whispered prayers and stared into the dark glamper until the sun peeked over the treetops, then rolled off the bench with a groan and tiptoed outside.

CHAPTER 5

Saturday

Piper wrapped a crocheted afghan around her shoulders and curled up in the lawn chair to marvel at the sunrise over the pine trees. The wind rustled through the leaves, and the call of a loon sounded through the forest. Piper sat up and cocked her ear to the side, waiting for the loon to call again and smiled at its loud cry.

"How beautiful!" she whispered while smiling at the bird's call. "Lord, you are amazing to create so many birds for us to enjoy." She leaned her head on the lawn chair and closed her eyes—half praying, half snoozing. When she opened them again, the bright colors of the sunrise had faded, and light flooded the campsite. Piper tiptoed into the glamper to grab the percolator.

"No need to tiptoe. I'm awake," Rosie said, peering down from the bunk in the pop-out roof. "What are you doing?"

"Lighting a fire and brewing coffee," Piper said and waved the empty percolator toward Rosie.

Rosie sat up and stretched, her red curls sticking out in every direction. She jumped down from the bunk and snatched the pot from Piper. "Not so fast, girlfriend. You'll burn the forest down with *your* fire-making skills."

"You don't trust me?" Piper asked.

"Where shall I begin?" Rosie marched out to the campfire ring. She wrinkled her nose and sniffed the air. "Do you smell cigarettes?" She glanced around the campsite.

"I did when I heard a noise in the middle of the night. I peeked out the window but didn't see anything."

Rosie leaned down and struck a match but jumped back and blew it out. "There's a cigarette in the ring." She pointed.

"Probably from the campers before us."

"Nope. I've lit at least three fires since we arrived, and that cigarette is on top of the wood from last night."

Piper rubbed her chin. "What does that mean?"

"Someone poked around our campsite since we went to bed—is what that means." Rosie stood with her hands on her hips, glaring. "Grab that notebook and write this down, would ya?"

Piper grinned. "A cigarette in our campfire ring isn't a clue about the Duchess' missing diamond."

"I know it's not, but it's weird, and we should document it."

Piper found the notebook on the counter and slipped back outside. "Rosie, are you sure we're safe out here in the woods?"

"Life isn't safe, my friend. But I'm fairly certain we're fine. Do you honestly think Mr. Grouchy Ranger wants anything yucky happening at his campground? No, we're fine." Rosie pushed the percolator over the fire and dropped into the chair next to Piper. "Did you write that down?" She pointed to the campfire.

Piper nodded. "Maybe I shouldn't leave you out here alone today. I have a weird feeling."

"One, I'm surrounded by fellow glampers and we have a full day planned. Two, you'd have to stay here and glamp with me because

I'm certainly not going to sit and listen to piano teacher stuff all day." Rosie grimaced and stuck out her tongue.

Piper laughed. "Your description sounds like psychological torture."

"Something like that," Rosie said. "I'm getting dressed. We can have coffee when I get back."

Piper nodded and closed her eyes, listening to the rustling trees.

Rosie popped out of the camper, and Piper grinned. "Goodness, friend—where did you find this ensemble?"

Rosie curtseyed and twirled. The purple shift dress with orange, pink, and green circles flashed in the sunshine. "You like?"

"It's you." Piper smiled.

Rosie pouted. "Well, I know what that means, but I don't care. I love it." She poured a mug of coffee and plopped into the chair next to Piper. "Why were you up so early?"

"Sun woke me up."

"Do you have a full day at the conference?"

"Yes, but it's the last day."

"Oh, good. Want to check out that museum and search for clues and find the Duchess' missing diamond?"

Piper sipped her coffee and stared into the woods. She turned to Rosie and smiled. "Sure."

"Deal," Rosie said. "I'll keep the notebook with me today in case anything strange happens. So about this diamond. You know the jewel is worth a boatload of cash. What will we do if we find it?" She tapped her lips. "I read a little about the Duchess—of course, she wasn't the Duchess yet when she vacationed here. The museum displays Liz's invitation to Wallis' first wedding. Her story is rather sad. Diamonds and jewels didn't give her lasting happiness, did they? I'd take the reward from the museum, though." Rosie laughed.

"How much?"

"Ten thousand."

Piper whistled. "That's enough to set you up in paint and canvases for the rest of your life."

Rosie laughed and tossed her red curls. "Or all the vintage clothing I can find." She spread the colorful fabric of her shift dress and winked at Piper.

"I love you and your crazy sense of style, my friend."

Rosie stood and curtseyed. "You're welcome. I'm practicing my curtseying for the Duchess."

"You know she's not alive, right?"

Rosie smiled. "Of course, but when the royal family calls us to England to thank us for recovering the diamond, I don't want to fall on my face when it's time to curtsey."

Piper laughed. "Hey, I'll text you if C# isn't at the conference today. Seems odd she left before she won her award last night."

Rosie stood and stretched. "Yeah, but she's always been the odd one."

Piper smiled at her 1960s-attired friend. "I guess we're all odd in our own way, right, Rosie?"

"Hey!" Rosie hollered. "I'm not odd—I'm one of a kind!"

Piper gave her friend a quick squeeze. "Be careful, okay? I don't like the idea of someone lurking around here."

Rosie saluted. "Aye aye, captain. Never you fear. I'll stay with the group and keep my eyes open."

Piper gave her a thumbs-up and hurried to her ride. "I'll see you later tonight."

As the hall filled with piano teachers, Piper glanced around. No sign of C#. She turned her attention to her teachers filling the row. All ten of her academy's piano instructors turned to her with a smile, notebooks in hand.

Piper looked forward to today's sessions—brainstorming round tables and time for her group to compare notes and discuss ideas. She wanted to hear what her teachers learned in the workshops they attended. She hoped everyone had new ideas to implement. But something in the back of her head sounded alarm bells. Something wasn't right, and her spine tingled.

---I don't see C# yet
---Well, her husband has already written me a ticket for a smoky fire.
---Sorry.

Someone slipped into the seat next to her. "Good morning, Miss Haydn."

Piper startled and placed her hand on her heart, her eyes wide. "Oh, Mr. Figsby—you scared me!"

He chuckled. "I don't usually have that effect on the ladies. My apologies."

"My mind is elsewhere."

His eyes narrowed. "Anything wrong?"

Piper crossed her arms. "Not really, but I have an odd feeling. Have you seen C# around?"

"That woman with the big hair and leather pants?" he asked. "Haven't seen her."

"Weren't you talking with her last night? After dinner?"

He rubbed the side of his nose and smiled at Piper. "Nope, wasn't me."

"I'm mistaken then," Piper said, but she made a mental note to add this tidbit to Rosie's investigation notebook. Scott Figsby and C# had definitely been in some sort of conversation last night—a heated one if their facial expressions and gestures meant anything. Then Carolyn disappeared.

"How many clients did you say you have?" he asked.

Piper narrowed her eyes. "Clients?"

He cleared his throat and pretended to cough. "I mean *students*."

Piper mumbled a number and inched her chair away from Scott. His expensive suit and Rolex said one thing about him, and his lie about talking to C# and calling students "clients" said another. She made a mental note. *Investigate Scott Figsby.*

Piper hurried through the conference hall to her next session: "Shostakovich and Censorship." The piano at the end of the hallway tempted her to stop. She hadn't played for days. She stretched her fingers and glanced at her watch. "Why listen to a lecture on Shostakovich when I can play one of his pieces?" she whispered, and a smile lit her face.

She dropped her notebook and bag onto the floor and sat on the bench. She stretched her fingers and played "Concerto No. 1" in C minor. Her fingers flew over the keys, and her breathing slowed. The piano calmed her soul. She finished the piece and slid the lid over the keys.

"Brava!" a voice behind her called out.

Her cheeks flushed—she hadn't expected an audience. Piper turned and gasped. "Mr. Figsby? Are you following me?" She stood and grabbed her things.

"Shostakovich, correct? Aren't you on your way to the session on him and Russian censorship?" He smiled.

"How do you know which session I signed up for?" Her heart beat faster, and she glanced around. No one moved in the hallways. She was alone with a man she barely knew—a man who knew too much and evaded her questions. She turned toward the lobby. "I need to grab something at the gift shop. Go ahead, and perhaps I'll catch up to you."

"No trouble. I'll go with you, and we can sneak in late together."

Piper held up her hand. "No. I'll go by myself. Good day, Mr. Figsby." She hurried to the lobby, contemplating what had upset her: something about the way he appeared out of nowhere and knew which session she signed up for. She shivered. "Probably nothing," she whispered. "Too much remembering my recital and Daniel." She quickened her pace and reached the lobby before her imagination got the best of her. She dropped into an overstuffed chair and stared at the floral painting on the wall. She willed her heartbeat to slow, but the icy finger of fear lodged firmly in her chest, and she fought an urge to abandon the conference and run back to her safe home in Cranberry Harbor.

"Piper," Anna said, sliding into the chair next to her. "Thank you for bringing me to the conference. I didn't think you would since I'm so new. Aren't you late for Shostakovich?"

"Yes, I am. What about you?"

Anna giggled. "I needed coffee." She held up a tall cup and rolled her eyes.

"That's exactly what I need. Where did you find that?"

Anna pointed across the lobby. "Here—take this. They gave me a coupon."

"Wait for me," Piper said. "We can sneak in late together." When she said this to her friend, the "Wait for me" wasn't creepy, but when the man she hardly knew demanded it, alarm bells derailed her calm and sent her running to find other humans. *Calm down, Piper. Your overactive imagination will get you into trouble one of these days.*

Piper and Anna snuck into the back of the Shostakovich workshop. The speaker wore a bow tie and thick black glasses. His hair parted down the middle reminded Piper of that guy on the popcorn ad.

She grinned and pulled out her notebook, hoping to learn about one of her favorite composers.

"Here we see his use of dissonance to push back at the accepted Soviet music of his time. His love for Western composers and willingness to use tonality in fresh ways upset the regime. The government censored Shostakovich."

Piper scribbled notes and covered the pages in her notebook with information. She loved history and music, and combining both in a lecture on a beloved composer filled her heart with happiness. She glanced up from her note-taking and scowled. Scott Figsby sat in the front row but turned, staring at her. She concentrated on the professor, but her mind raced with questions and her heart pounded. She flipped open a new page in her notebook and wrote what she knew about Scott Figsby. She tried to concentrate on the speaker, but if she didn't write the thoughts swirling in her mind, she wouldn't sort out why the man upset her.

She wrote in columns.

*From Stevens Point

*Teaches piano

*Handsome sharp dresser

*Piano degree from UW-Stout

*Calls students "clients"

*Talking to C#

*Says he wasn't talking to C#

*Followed me down the hall in the hotel

*Likes to appear out of nowhere

*Rosie says she met a Scott with a similar description.

*Same guy? How?

How can I get a picture of him to show Rosie?

"And so his silence on the matter leaves questions. Was he a devoted Communist, or was he something else? Thank you."

The audience applauded, and Piper shut the notebook. Her list hadn't calmed her racing mind, and she had missed half of the lecture she wanted to hear. She dug her phone from her bag and snapped a picture of Scott while Anna talked to someone in the row in front of them. She slid her phone into her purse and tapped Anna.

"I'm going back for more coffee. Do you need anything?"

"No thanks. I'll catch up to you later," Anna said and returned to her conversation.

Piper hurried to the lobby. She wished Rosie were here to observe him. Rosie would ferret out Mr. Figsby's inconsistencies in thirty seconds. Piper sometimes teased her zany, colorful friend, but Rosie was as close as a sister to her. She loved her friend, and together they made an excellent team.

---Got another ticket from the pleasant forest ranger. You'll never guess why.

Piper tried to imagine another legitimate reason for a ticket. She rubbed her temple.

--- I have zero idea. What did you do?
---I didn't do anything!
---Well? What happened?

Piper watched the bubbles in the messaging app waiting for Rosie's reply. The barista slid a cup across the counter.

"Your coffee, miss."

"Thank you," Piper said and picked up the cup. She turned back to the counter. "Excuse me. I have a weird question, but have you heard anything about the park rangers being extra insistent on the rules out at Peninsula State Park?"

The barista laughed. "At Pen Park? No. They're usually really chill. My brother and his friends threw a loud underage party last week, and the ranger only told them to keep it down. I'd say they're too lenient if anything. He should have gotten a ticket for that, or at least a call to my parents."

Piper bit her lip. "Okay, forget I asked." She smiled and dropped a tip into the jar.

"Thanks," she said. "There *is* a new ranger out there who's a grouch, but she's not bad when you talk to her. Hope that helps."

"Definitely. Thank you for your time." Piper sipped the coffee and dropped into a chair to sort out the new information and the questions swirling in her mind.

She checked her phone for Rosie's reply.

      ---He wrote us a ticket for the cigarette in the fire ring and found one by the road.

      ---What? How did he even know they were there?

      ---Exactly.

      ---How much do we owe right now? I'll pay for it, of course.

      ---I'll add them up later. Gotta go.

      ---K

"Something is rotten in Door County," Piper whispered. She stared out the window at the water, waiting for the calm to seep into her mind, but questions churned, and peace seemed far away.

"Why did you take my picture?" Scott Figsby dropped into the chair across the table from Piper.

Piper's eyebrows narrowed. "What are you talking about?"

He glanced at her phone and up into her eyes. He stared like a parent waiting for a confession from an errant child.

Piper raised her chin and stared down her nose as she dropped the phone into her Chanel bag. "What I do on my phone is my business. Excuse me." She walked past him, her head held high, but her heartbeat pounded in her ears.

Scott yanked her elbow, and she pulled it away. "Do not touch me," she said through clenched teeth.

He stood and waved his hands in the air. "Whoa. Calm down. I wanted to know if my gorgeous body and charming disposition overcame you. I figured you snapped a picture to remember my handsome face." He grinned.

Piper stepped back, creating a distance between them. "Have you seen Carolyn?"

"Carolyn who?" he turned his head to the side and stared at her.

"Sharpe. I saw her talking to you," Piper said.

He smiled. "All the ladies want to talk to me. What can I say? But as for this person, Carolyn? No idea. Hope you find her."

"So do I. Good day, Mr. Figsby," she said and breezed past him into the lobby. *How does he always find me, and how would he know I took that picture?* He hadn't done anything illegal, but his hovering and constant presence left her with more questions than answers. She needed to determine if he was bizarre or creepy, but she had a piano teachers conference to attend and teachers to debrief—no time for figuring out why Scott Figsby gave her the creeps.

The coffee warmed Piper and eased her mind. She held the hot cup and sipped while making her way to the restaurant to meet her teachers and discuss what they had learned at the conference. The sessions ended this afternoon, and they would spend the evening at a banquet and piano concert by renowned pianist Isadore Renaldi. Tomorrow she and Rosie would explore Door County and stop at the orchards to do market research for her father. They would drive home on Monday, and thankfully she would never see Scott Figsby again. He was handsome. She gave him that, but something seemed off.

She found an empty table in the restaurant and dropped into a chair. Her fingers tapped on the table, and her heart raced. Her mind swirled with questions.

Anna slid into a chair across from Piper. She reached out and patted Piper's hand. "You okay, boss?"

Piper rubbed her eyes and smiled. "Too much on my mind, but yes. How were the sessions?"

Anna's eyes lit up, and she opened her notebook. "I learned so much. Thank you for this opportunity. The speaker said her biggest success came when she added games and flashcards to lessons. I'll give her ideas a try with my students. What do you think?"

"Hmm?"

"Earth to Piper," Anna said and waved her hand in front of Piper's eyes.

Piper blinked. "Forgive me. What were you saying?"

"I'm going to implement their tips with my students. I believe they'll respond well." She tapped her music print notebook. "I gathered so many ideas. My brain is tired, but I'll review my notes when I get home."

"I'm glad you came."

"Can I ask you something, Piper?"

"Of course."

"What led to opening your academy?"

Piper smiled. "I taught in my home studio for several years, but I always dreamed of opening a center to teach all the arts—or as many as fit in the building. You know I'm all about the piano, but when I walk through the halls and hear a child practicing guitar, then walk past a class learning tap, or see Rosie painting with a room full of four-year-olds, my heart sings. The academy is my dream come true." Piper's eyes sparkled, and the tension in her shoulders slipped away. "When the town replaced the old school, I worked with the city, and my dad, to purchase the building and opened the academy. I am so proud of our accomplishments."

"You've done such a great job. I love working at the academy," Anna said.

"The gang's all here." Susan dropped her bags onto the table and plopped into a chair. "Piper, thanks for bringing us. The sessions are fabulous. I've learned so much my head is swimming."

"Same," Ellis said.

Piper pointed to their notebooks. "Tell me something you learned."

Her teachers went around the table, sharing tidbits and stories from their sessions.

Piper jotted notes and smiled as they shared. Bringing her piano teachers to the conference worked out well, and her academy would benefit from the excitement and fresh ideas.

"Well, we have one more session, the banquet, and the concert. I'm so glad everything worked out for you to take part. I hope this becomes a yearly tradition. See you when we get ready for dinner?"

"Five o'clock in our hotel room?" Anna asked.

Piper nodded. "I'll find you. Thanks for letting me dress in your room."

The ladies collected their bags and notebooks and hurried down the hall. Piper checked her schedule. Her last workshop wasn't exciting—a summary of the conference—she might skip the session and use the time to untangle her mind and calm the worry buzzing around Scott Figsby and the missing C#.

Her phone dinged.

> *---Are you surviving, honey?*
> *---I'm ok, Mom.*
> *---Do you need a spa day when you get home?*
> *---LOL. It's not that bad, Mom. But don't tell Rosie.*
> *---Ok. See you soon.*

Piper grinned. Sarah Haydn knew her daughter well. All the outdoor time *was* a bit much for her, but she was surviving, and if her presence in the glamper made her best friend happy, then the entire experience was a win-win.

> ---*Hey, investigating the diamond. Guess what?*
> ---*What?*
> ---*Maybe an inside job.*
> ---*How did you hear that tidbit?*
> ---*Fill you in tonight.*
> ---*OK*

What are the odds that a British duchess vacationed in Door County, befriended a local, and gave her a diamond that was stolen? Pretty far-fetched if you ask me. She would have Rosie take her to the museum tomorrow, and they would poke around, but Piper knew nothing would come of it. Someone would have solved this mystery decades ago if it were true. She slung her bag over her shoulder and walked to the lobby. She wanted to step outside and check the air temperature. She hoped to find a pleasant breeze and an empty rocker on the porch. She would count the sailboats on the lake and allow the water and fresh air to calm her soul. Something to ease her mind. *Maybe I'm too worked up because of things in the past. I need to concentrate on the happiness and success of today. Lord, can you calm my mind? Help me trust in you.*

She dropped into a rocker at the corner of the porch surrounding the restaurant. When the lake breeze ruffled her hair, she untied the music-print silk scarf from her neck and wrapped the fabric around her hair. She donned her Fendi shades to keep from squinting and leaned her head on the rocker's back. She pushed her toes against the floor to move the chair and soon settled into a rhythmic pace. Between the rocking and the sound of the waves, the tight coil inside her chest unwound. Rocking on the porch of a fancy hotel and listening to the water—bliss. *Everything will work out—nothing to worry about.* She took a deep breath and blew the air out.

"What a gigantic sigh! You okay?"

Piper opened one eye and stared into the face of Scott Figsby. She sat up and whipped her sunglasses off.

"Why are you following me?"

He raised his hands in front of her. "Whoa, girl! I'm being friendly."

Piper gathered her belongings and walked away from Scott.

"Where are you going?" he called.

"I have a concert to attend," she said and hurried into the hotel, her heart beating and her mind churning—again.

Piper slipped into the room several of her piano teachers shared in the hotel to get dressed for the evening banquet and concert. "You girls are living the good life here. I'm excited to take a hot shower."

Giggles followed her into the bathroom, and Anna called, "Take all the time you need in there, boss!"

Hot water ran over her hair, and Piper relaxed. If she didn't need to hurry, she would run a bath and soak away the three days in the camper—*excuse me, "glamper."* The hot water worked out the kinks in her muscles, but her mind swirled with questions about Scott Figsby. *Is he socially awkward? Or does his odd behavior mean something more?*

Piper slipped into her navy blue evening dress and hollered, "Can I get some zipper help in here, please?"

"Of course," Ellis hurried in, hot rollers in her hair and a tube of lipstick in her hand. She tugged Piper's zipper closed. "Pretty dress, Piper."

"Thanks. Does this scarf work with the color?" Piper wrapped a cream-colored floral print scarf around her shoulders and tucked the ends around her elbows. She twirled in a circle.

"Beautiful. Where did you find the scarf?" Ellis reached out and rubbed the hem between her fingers. "It's so soft."

"My mom found it at the Getty Museum."

"Wow—I love it! Completes your outfit." Ellis leaned over the sink and swiped lipstick over her lips. "Everyone getting ready in here together reminds me of college. How many roommates did you have, Piper?"

"Three, but one left mid-semester."

Ellis nodded. "You went to Juilliard?"

Piper nodded and fluffed her hair.

"What was that like?"

"Demanding and exhilarating all at the same time. I appreciated the opportunity, but I'm glad those days are past." She smiled at Ellis. "I enjoy being my own boss."

"And ours." Ellis nudged her with her shoulder.

"Exactly." Piper giggled.

"What's so funny in here, ladies?" Anna breezed in with her toothbrush and nudged between the girls. "Come on—some of us have more work to do to get pretty than others."

Ellis rolled her eyes and Piper laughed.

Piper sat on the bed to slip into her heels. "Have any of you noticed that guy that's always around?"

"The guy you ate with the other night?"

"Yeah."

"Not really. I saw him in a workshop and Professor Werth's session. I also noticed him arguing with your little friend in the hallway yesterday."

"My little friend?"

"You know," Betsy said. "The loud one that yelled at you."

"Oh, brother," Piper said. "She goes by 'C#.'"

Anna poked her head out of the bathroom. "What's with that name? What adult calls themselves something so silly?"

"Why doesn't she like you?" Ellis asked.

Piper slid the strap of her sandal through the tiny silver buckle and stood to smooth her skirt. "I have no idea, ladies. C# has hated me for decades, and I'm not quite certain what I did to deserve her wrath. Speaking of C#, has anyone seen her around today?"

Anna rolled her eyes and said, "Thankfully, no."

Piper stared out the window at the water. She watched a boat glide past and took a deep breath before turning back to her friends. "Something feels off, and I'm unsure what to think."

Ellis picked up her purse and room key. "Let your mind rest. We have a delicious banquet and a beautiful concert to enjoy tonight."

"You're right. Thanks." She smiled at Ellis and followed her into the hall.

"I'll catch up!" Anna called as the door clicked behind them.

Piper and Ellis made their way to the table reserved for Haydn Music Academy.

"All the way in the back?" Ellis whined.

Piper settled into her chair and smiled. "I don't mind. I can keep my eyes on everything without appearing nosy."

"You're that nervous?"

"I can't explain, Ellis. I have questions, and things don't add up. Plus, the ranger out at the park keeps ticketing Rosie and me. I'm ready to get back to my old Victorian house and finish wallpapering my turret. I want to get back to my people . . . and my bed."

"I need a cup of Ruby's coffee and something from Sweetberry's," Ellis said.

"My sentiments exactly." Piper winked at Ellis and checked her phone, but no new messages. She texted Rosie.

---Everything ok out there?

The table filled with her instructors, and Piper beamed as she glanced at the smiling women filling the seats. They sat around her table as her employees, but she considered them friends. All her hard work, planning, and rehabilitating the old schoolhouse had been worth the work.

Life is good. A smile spread across her face as Isadore Renaldi played the opening notes of the Shostakovich "Waltz No. 2," She closed her eyes, and the music calmed her churning mind. *It's fine. Everything's fine. You're imagining things, Piper. Enjoy the concert and the meal and let your frivolous worries go.*

The deep notes of the final piece faded, and the audience applauded. Piper stood with the crowd and clapped her hands. The music calmed her mind, and she was ready for a good night's rest and a day of exploring Door County with Rosie.

Anna hugged her. "Thank you for bringing us along for the conference. And paying for us."

Piper gave each of them a hug. "See you next week, ladies. I can't wait to see how what we've learned here affects our students. I have to run and catch my ride to the campground. See you."

They waved, and Piper hurried through the hotel to meet her ride at the main entrance, squeezing into the backseat just in time. She leaned her head on the window and closed her eyes. The conference was over, and she wouldn't see Scott Figsby or C# daily anymore. Their presence had added to her anxiety. Swirling thoughts kicked in when she considered the two people who contributed to an odd experience at the conference. She watched the dark scenery pass by and tried to nail down what bothered her. Lightning cracked in the sky, startling Piper. She gasped and bolted upright in the car's backseat. "There's no piano program at UW-Stout," she whispered. "Scott said he got his degree at Stout. He called students clients." Her heart pounded, and the twinge of a headache wrapped around her skull. *That's why something seemed off. He lied to me.*

---Rosie, you'll never guess what I realized.

She scrolled through her messages and bit the inside of her cheek. Rosie hadn't replied hours earlier when Piper asked if everything was okay. Piper watched the screen, waiting for the bubbles to appear to show Rosie answering her text message. Nothing. The tightness in her chest reappeared, and the headache squeezed her skull. She blew out a breath and willed the driver to hurry. She needed to compare notes with Rosie. Maybe she would convince her to stay somewhere else. Piper scrolled through the local houses for rent and found one available in Sister Bay. She saved Beach Road Cottage in the app and dropped her phone into her purse. She would force Rosie to stay in actual accommodations for their last couple of nights. Her sanity needed a break from sleeping in the woods and suffering the park ranger's accusations. Time for a return to normalcy. Starting with a couple of nights out of the glamper. *Please, God—let Rosie agree.*

The car pulled up to their dark campsite, and Piper frowned. She shut the car door and waved as the car pulled away.

"I thought those lights were solar," she whispered, digging in her purse for her phone. She switched on the flashlight app and pointed it at the ground. She didn't need to end the night tripping over a tree root or stepping in a hole in the ground. "Rosie!" she called. "Turn the lights on!"

She trudged across the parking spot at the end of the campsite and held her light toward the glamper. The light shone on a mound of dirt around the campfire ring and a lump outside the fire pit. Piper gathered her skirt around her knees to avoid catching her dress on fire. *How did a log fall outside the fire pit? What's going on here, Rosie?*

She stepped closer to the fire pit to check on any remaining embers and see if she needed to go for water to put the fire out when she tripped. The log stuck out farther than she realized. She swung the light toward the fire pit, and her stomach clenched. Her eyes widened, and tears sprang to her eyes.

"Not again. Oh, not again." Her heart pounded, and she stifled a wail. A shoe connected to a leg lay outside the fire pit, and a body slumped over the bricks into the ring. The arm stretched in front of the face kept her from identifying the person. She ran to the glamper and slammed the door open. "Rosie, Rosie—we have to get out of here!"

She kicked off her heels and slid into the sandals by the bench she slept on last night. "Rosie!" she called and hoisted herself up into the pop-out in the camper's top. "Rosie, wake up! We have to get out of here!" She hit the blankets to wake Rosie, but Rosie wasn't in the bed. She jumped down and shone her light around the dark camper. Rosie wasn't in the front seat, and Rosie wasn't lying on the bench bed. Dishes lay on the floor, and blankets and clothing were piled on the table. The mini-fridge door flopped open, and the stove door hung crooked under the sink.

Piper yanked her phone from her purse and punched 9-1-1, but the call wouldn't go through. "Come on!" she yelled. Her heart pounded and her mind raced. "Where is Rosie?" she whispered. The lump in her throat gave way, and she sobbed. "This is too soon, God. Too soon. I said I didn't want to deal with anything like this again. I can't do this." She didn't want to go outside and be with the body. *Is it a body? What if he's breathing?* But sitting inside the glamper made her a sitting duck if anyone returned. She tried to redial 9-1-1 but still had no connection.

She pulled up the rental house she had saved and breathed a sigh of relief when the Internet worked. She booked the cottage and read the instructions. Now she needed a ride. *Internet, please hold on long enough for my Uber app to connect.* Her fingers trembled while she tried to book a ride, and tears rolled down her cheeks. She would call 9-1-1 when she got to the rental house. *Why does this keep happening to me?* She slid to the floor of the glamper, and a piece of purple fabric with orange, pink, and green circles caught her eye. The material hung from a cupboard hinge with a jagged tear down one side. "Who took you, Rosie?" she whispered as her heart hammered in her chest and her mind slid into despair.

CHAPTER 6

Sunday, midnight

The driver chattered, but Piper closed her eyes and leaned on the window. The pounding in her chest left her breathless, and her head ached. She punched 9-1-1 on her phone, ready to hang up again, but a voice came through the line.

"Door County 9-1-1. What's the address of your emergency?"

Piper's dry throat ached. She swallowed over a lump. "I don't know the street address. It's at the park."

"Which park, ma'am?"

"The state park. I need to report a body and a missing person."

The driver's eyes stared at Piper in the rearview mirror and widened. Piper put her finger to her lips.

"You're calling to report a body and a missing person? Where?"

"At Peninsula State Park. Site 232." Piper's voice trembled, and her stomach twisted. "Confirming a body at site 232 at Peninsula State Park?"

"Yes."

"What phone number are you calling from?"

Piper's voice trembled. "920-555-1212."

"Tell me exactly what happened."

The lump in Piper's throat grew, and she choked back a sob. "I returned from the piano teachers conference to a dark campsite. When I walked to the camper, I tripped on a log at the fire pit, but . . ." She squeezed her eyes shut, willing away this nightmare. "I tripped on a leg."

"Are you with the body now?"

"No, I'm in a car on my way to a rental cottage."

"Is he awake? Breathing?"

"I don't know!" Piper shouted.

"Tell me why you think he's dead. Is he beyond help?"

"I panicked, all right? I don't know if he was breathing, but he seemed dead because he was lying face down in the fire pit."

"How far are you from the campground, ma'am?"

Piper glanced at the Uber driver. He held up his hand and flashed five fingers twice.

"Ten miles," she told the dispatcher.

"I didn't have a signal, but my app worked for a ride. I've tried calling over and over, and this is the first time my call went through." The shock of discovering the body and the worry over Rosie's whereabouts chilled Piper. Her teeth chattered, and goosebumps rose on her bare arms. "Can you turn the heat on, please?" she asked the driver.

He nodded, his eyes still wide. When the hot air blew to the back seat, Piper leaned back and concentrated on the dispatcher's questions.

"Can you identify the body?"

"I'm not sure."

"What's the address of the cottage you're renting?"

"334 Beach Road."

"Your name?"

"Piper Haydn."

"Who is missing?"

"My friend Roosevelt Hale."

Piper answered each question with a calm voice, but she willed the driver to hurry. She needed to slam the door behind her and lock out everything frightening and wicked.

"Is he in danger? Ma'am. Is he in danger?"

"Who?"

"Roosevelt."

Piper rubbed the spot between her eyebrows and sighed. "Roosevelt is a girl. My friend Rosie."

"Describe her."

Piper's mind whirled with memories of Rosie. Rosie grabbing her hand and running to the swings on her first day at Cranberry Harbor Elementary. Rosie twirling through her foyer, faking martial arts moves. Rosie's laugh.

"Ma'am?"

"Ummm. She has red curly hair." Piper's head swam, and spots floated in front of her eyes. "She's short and thin. She wore a purple dress with orange, pink, and green circles the last time I saw her. She hung out with the other glampers today." Tears pressed behind Piper's eyes.

"Glampers?"

"Fancy camping or something like that. I saw her when I left for the piano teachers conference at eight this morning and haven't seen her since."

"So you don't know when she went missing or who the body is?"

The questions stabbed Piper's heart, and guilt filled her mind. "No. No, I don't know."

"We have dispatched police and an ambulance to the park. Stay at the cottage and keep your phone on, Piper. The police will want to speak with you."

"I will," her voice squeaked, and the line disconnected.

The man in the front seat cleared his throat. "Did you say—?"

"Yes," cut in Piper. "Please. I can't talk about this right now."

He nodded, and Piper stared into the moonless night. *Why does this keep happening to me? I don't understand.*

Piper realized waving off the Uber driver was a mistake approximately ten seconds after his lights disappeared down Beach Road. Her hands trembled as she pointed her phone at the door's keypad. Crickets chirped, and waves lapped the shore, but Piper's heart pounded, and when she punched the code into the pad, the door clicked open into a dark house. Piper ran in, twisted the deadbolt, and slid to the ground, choking back a sob. Tree branches scratched the window, and Piper jumped. Tears ran down her cheeks, and she wadded a tissue between her fingers. "This cannot keep happening," she whispered. She stared at the shelves ahead, her eyes glazing over as she stared. "Where are you, Rosie?"

The ticking clock grew louder, and the scratching branches stretched Piper's nerves taut. She pulled the curtains and checked the deadbolt again. She sat on the white leather sofa, her feet planted firmly on the ground, and stared into the dark house. She tried to slow her breathing, but her heart hammered in her chest and adrenaline coursed through her system. She picked at the tissue and wiped her nose. Her head pounded, and her mind shouted impossible questions. She would *not* let her mind dwell on why she sat alone in a dark Airbnb in Door County. She would figure out how to get out of here without getting entangled in the investigation. She had to. "Why me?" She swallowed a whimper. "Stop it, Piper. Calm down and think straight. Get out of here."

Moonlight shone through the kitchen windows and lit a path across the rooms. Piper moved out of the light and stared into the darkness. She rubbed her arms and attempted to focus, but her thoughts bounced around like the ball in a pinball machine. She concentrated on her breathing, walked to the desk, and picked up the welcome binder. "The story of Beach Road Cottage"—she read the words written across the front. Piper ran her hand over the words and settled into a chair near the curtained sliding glass doors. She turned her phone light on and read, "See what the Lord has done!"

"Lord, I will not say you have done this. Can't you see I'm not strong enough to face another murder?" A tear trickled down her cheek as a verse she memorized in Sunday School came to mind.

Have not I commanded thee? Be strong and of a good courage; be not afraid, neither be thou dismayed: for the Lord thy God is with thee whithersoever thou goest.

"Are you here, God? Are you actually here? Because I don't feel you. I feel scared and confused, and I'm angry you let this happen around me again. I'm scared for Rosie, and I'm not strong enough to go through another murder investigation. Please fix this, God."

Piper paced in the dark living room. Her body cried for sleep, but her mind wouldn't rest. She needed to call someone. *Who?* Will Maxwell's kind smile flashed in her mind. She and Cranberry Harbor's chief of police had a tenuous friendship. His cocky attitude and teasing habit annoyed her. But then, of course, he had saved her life a few months ago.

She should call her parents, but they would react too strongly to a 2:00 a.m. phone call. Same with her older brother, Braden, especially if she woke his children. Lenny—her dad's attorney—might pick up, but he would charge a premium. She dropped onto the couch and stared at her phone. The only voice Piper wanted to hear right now was Rosie's. Surely she had a reasonable explanation for disappearing and ignoring her phone and texts. Right?

Piper's eyes burned, but she didn't sleep. She needed answers to all the questions slamming around her mind. She searched her purse for her music print notebook and flipped it open to a blank page. "Okay, Rosie. I'm writing everything in a notebook. Let's figure this out."

She scribbled her muddled thoughts in the notebook.

*Rosie missing

* Torn fabric in glamper

* Scott Figsby following me

* Who is dead at our campsite?

* Where is C#?

* Rosie not answering her phone or texts

* Grouchy ranger?

She tossed the notebook onto the coffee table. Nothing made sense, and writing everything down hadn't revealed any clues to her frozen mind. The clock above the fireplace chimed three times. "Three a.m. and the police haven't come for me yet. I should rest." She lay down on the couch and pulled a fluffy blanket over her shoulders. The wind blew and a limb scratched at the window, but her eyes closed, and fitful sleep finally won. She tossed and turned and mumbled in her sleep, chasing an elusive Rosie in her dreams. Piper ran down street after street, Rosie's purple skirt disappearing around corners, never stopping no matter how many times Piper hollered, "Rosie!" She ran to Rosie's studio and pounded on the door for hours, but Rosie never answered.

Piper bolted upright. She rubbed her eyes and ran her fingers through her hair. The knocking wasn't in her dream—someone was pounding at the front door.

"Piper Haydn—police. Open up."

The insistent knock echoed through the house, and Piper pulled the blanket around her shoulders as she jumped off the couch. "I'm coming!" she hollered. She twisted the lock and pulled open the door. "I'm sorry. I was . . ." she trailed off, and her eyebrows rose. "What are *you* doing here?"

Will Maxwell leaned against the door frame, his deep brown eyes searching hers. He ran his fingers through his hair and blew out a breath. "Miss Haydn, you're in a heap of trouble. May I come in?"

Piper stepped aside, and Chief Maxwell stepped in. He stood in the entryway and glanced around the room. "More space than Rosie's glamper, huh?"

Piper nodded.

"You know I have questions?"

She nodded again. "Come sit down. Might as well tell you everything."

He followed her to the living room and perched on one end of the couch while Piper crossed the living room and curled up in the opposite corner.

"Miss Haydn, you should not have left the campground. Leaving made you appear guilty."

"Call me, Piper, Chief Maxwell. And I panicked when the call to 9-1-1 didn't go through. The Uber app worked, so I booked a ride and came here. I told the dispatcher where I went, and obviously I'm not hiding—you're here. Why *are* you here?"

"The Door County sheriff called after they searched your name. She's sending someone to talk to you soon, so I can't talk to you about the case. I'm here as your friend."

Piper's head jerked up and tears filled her eyes. She picked at the fluffy white blanket. "No, you're not. Not really. If I say the wrong thing or you find out I committed a crime, you'll do your job no matter what."

He frowned and stood. "I'll brew tea." He disappeared into the kitchen, and Piper took a deep breath as a tear trickled down her cheek. She realized that what she said was true. Will Maxwell was a man of integrity, and he would arrest her in a heartbeat if she confessed—not that she *had* anything to confess. She sniffled and listened to the sounds of the teakettle on the stove. Will cleared his throat in the other room, and Piper thought of those brown eyes, his smile, and that deep voice. She shuddered. *No. I'm not interested in Chief Maxwell.*

He handed her a steaming mug of tea and sat on the other end of the couch.

"Thank you, Chief Maxwell," she said and blew across the mug to cool the hot liquid. Her hands soaked up the heat, and warmth crept up her arms, but the tea didn't thaw the chill in her spirit.

"Will." .

"Hmm?"

"I said call me Will," the chief said.

"I can't. It sounds disrespectful to me—sorry."

"Not if I *asked* you to call me by my first name." He leaned forward and rested his elbow on his knee, watching her.

"I'll try. No promises." Piper took a sip of the spicy tea. "Mmm. Thank you."

He pointed to the notebook on the coffee table. "What's that?"

Piper reached for the notebook and flipped to her notes. "The first pages contain my notes from the piano teachers conference. Here." She pointed to her scribbles at the back of the spiral notebook. "This is my jumbled thoughts about some strange happenings over the week."

His eyes lit up, but he sat back on the couch. "Don't tell me anything. Wait for the police."

She watched him for a moment. His eyes wandered to her notebook, and he glanced away.

He wants to know what's in there. Piper smiled and flipped slowly through the pages. She glanced at him every few seconds. He watched her with his eyebrows raised.

"You're taunting me now, Miss Haydn."

She dropped the notebook on the table. "You want to know what's in there?"

He ran his fingers through his dark hair and blew out a breath. "Of course I do, but this isn't my investigation, and I'm here strictly as a friendly face for you."

She nodded. "I see. Well, my notes don't solve anything. Nothing about Rosie." She bit her lip, and a tear trickled down her cheek. "I'm scared for her."

The chief nodded. "I am too." He glanced at his watch and checked his phone. "I wish they'd hurry and question you."

Piper's stomach twisted as she watched Chief Maxwell. What did his fear mean for Rosie's safe return? The fear she had held back crashed over her, and tears rolled down her cheeks.

"Hey." The chief sat next to her and took the cup of tea. He set it on the table, then pulled a blanket from the chest near the couch. "Hey—don't cry," he whispered. He wrapped the blanket around Piper's shoulders. "We'll find her." He pulled Piper into his arms, and she melted against his muscular chest.

She collapsed against him as tears ran down her face, and a headache pounded behind her eyes. She leaned her head against the police chief and let go of all her fears. His arms tightened around her, and he leaned his head on hers. "You must have been so scared. I'm sorry."

She nodded against him, and a ragged sigh escaped. He wiped the hair away from her eyes. "You need to lie down and rest. You're tired." He gathered pillows from the corners of the couch and covered her with a blanket, then turned off the lights. "I'll wake you when the police come. Get some sleep."

Piper closed her eyes. Her fear for Rosie still hammered in her chest. The terror at finding another body hadn't disappeared—worries about the police questioning lodged in her heart. But Chief Maxwell was right. She *needed* rest. She drifted to sleep, and for some strange reason her dreams weren't nightmares of her missing friend or of the body she had discovered. No, she dreamed of a charming brown-eyed man with graying curls at his temples. Piper smiled in her sleep.

Chapter 7

Sunday morning

"Hey, Piper." A hand tapped her shoulder, and she squeezed her eyes shut against the light. "The Door County police are on their way. You might want to pull yourself together. Coffee's almost done."

Piper pushed herself off the pillow and sat up. Her dry eyes burned from crying, and her muscles ached. "What time is it?" She stretched her arms above her head and yawned. "Did they hear from Rosie?"

"I'm sorry. Nothing from Rosie. It's seven-thirty." He handed her a mug.

The steam swirled up, and Piper gulped the hot liquid. She needed something to banish the exhaustion from her brain or she would never keep her eyes open during her interrogation. Chief Maxwell leaned against the door frame, his eyes wide.

"What?"

"I've never seen a girl drink a cup of coffee that fast."

"Well, I need to wake up, Chief Maxwell. Is there more?"

"Yes—let me grab a refill for you." He took her mug and hurried into the kitchen. "Do you drink it black for real?"

"When I can't get a latte at Ruby's, I sure do." Piper ran her fingers through her hair and tugged the floral print scarf off her shoulders. Her blue evening dress scratched her skin. "I can't believe I slept in this."

Will handed her the mug and winked. "You're mighty spiffy, Miss Haydn."

Piper blushed and turned away from his gaze. "I arrived at the campsite after a banquet and concert." She clamped her lips together and tears stung her eyes.

"I know," he whispered. "You didn't think to change."

She nodded.

"Better peek in the mirror before they arrive," he suggested.

Piper gulped the coffee and stood on shaky legs. She wobbled to the mirror and groaned. "Oh, my." Her hair stood on end from all the hairspray she used last night and mascara smudged under her eyes. Wrinkles from the pillow creased her cheek and a crust of something lined her jaw. She hurried to the bathroom to force her hair and face into some sort of order.

"They're here!" Chief Maxwell called from the living room. Piper stared into the mirror and gulped air.

You can do this, Piper. She squared her shoulders before facing the music—Chopin's Funeral March, in this case.

The officers rose from the leather couch when she walked into the living room. "Miss Haydn, sit." The taller officer pointed to the empty cushion on the end, and Piper plopped onto it, her knees giving out at the last moment. She held her breath and glanced between the two officers. Chief Maxwell sat in a chair, out of Piper's sight.

"Where were you last night?" The other officer flipped open a notebook and scribbled notes.

"I attended a piano teachers conference until late in the evening. I rode back to the park with some other campers attending the conference."

"What time did you return?" The tall officer peered at her over the top of his glasses.

"Eleven thirty, I think."

"You think?"

"I checked the time right before my ride dropped me off."

"They didn't stay?"

"No. They stopped, I hopped out, and they went on their way. No one wanted to chat that late at night."

"So you saw the body first thing?" The short officer scribbled and the taller officer asked questions.

"No. The lights strung around the campsite weren't on. That was odd. Rosie always left them on."

"What did you do?"

"I walked carefully so I wouldn't trip and I called for my friend Rosie."

The officer flipped back through his notebook. "You said her name is Roosevelt?"

"Yes, Roosevelt Hale, but she goes by Rosie."

"Did she answer when you called?"

"No." Piper bit her cheek to stop the tears welling in her eyes.

"Then?"

"Then I kept watching for things so I wouldn't trip. When I got near the campfire ring, I tripped on a log, but . . ." She covered her face.

"What did you trip over?"

"A leg."

"A leg? You didn't see a body?"

"I only noticed the foot and leg at first. The clothes seemed to belong to a man. There wasn't a real fire, only embers."

"Go on," the tall officer said.

"I ran to the camper yelling for Rosie and checked her bunk. She wasn't in her bunk or mine. I stepped over piles—stuff everywhere. When I sat on the floor to gather my thoughts, I found a ripped piece of fabric stuck in the cupboard hinge—a piece of the dress she was wearing yesterday."

The officer nodded and scribbled. "How long did you stay there?"

"Five minutes? I don't know." Piper rubbed her eyes and took a deep breath. Chill bumps rose on her arms and her stomach ached as she relived the night before.

"You sat on the camper floor for five minutes and then?"

"My phone wouldn't connect to 9-1-1, so I ran outside. He lay face down in the ring. I'm not sure who he is." She covered her eyes and shuddered.

"If you guessed?" The short officer stared at Piper, his pen poised, ready to write.

"Scott Figsby," she mumbled.

"Who? I need you to speak up, Miss Haydn."

"Scott Figsby."

"Who is Scott Figsby?" The officer scribbled notes as she talked.

Piper rubbed her eyes. "I met him at the piano teachers conference. At first I enjoyed talking to him. He was a little flirty and friendly. Nothing serious. We ate dinner together one evening and ran into each other during different presentations."

"Did you exchange contact information with him?"

"No," Piper said. "As the conference went on, I worried he was stalking me. I don't know." She rubbed her temple to clear the fuzzy thoughts threading through her mind.

"Stalking?"

"He was at the coffee shop, the hallway, and the rockers on the porch. His constant presence and false familiarity seemed odd."

"Did you report this to anyone?"

"No. I knew I would never see him again."

"Where did you say he's from?"

"He *said* Stevens Point."

"What do you mean by 'He said'?"

"Well, he also called his piano students *clients* and said he studied piano pedagogy at the University of Wisconsin-Stout."

The officer watched her for a moment. "So?"

Piper straightened her spine and leaned forward. "UW-Stout doesn't offer a piano program. Why would he lie? That and piano teachers teach *students*, not clients."

The officer scribbled. "Do you think he lied about his name?"

"I don't know. Have you found Rosie?"

The tall officer shook his head. Piper's stomach lurched, and she pinched the bridge of her nose.

"We are searching the park and have officers at the exits."

"But what if they took her outside of the park already?" Panic pounded in her heart and a headache squeezed her temples. "Find her." Her voice rose. "Please."

"We're doing everything we can. Now back to last evening. We identified the person in your fire pit as a park ranger. Is that the person who followed you at the conference?"

Piper jumped from the couch, her heart pounded, and her eyes darted around the room. Her breath came in short bursts and she rested her hand on her throat. "I need a break. Can I please have a break?"

The tall officer stared at her over his glasses. "Fine. Ten minutes. You can walk around outside, but leave your phone here." He pointed to the table and Piper dropped her phone where he pointed.

She fled to the door, slamming it behind her. Cool air blew through the trees and leaves swirled around her feet. She dropped onto the swing in the front yard of the cottage and pushed her foot in the grass. She stared into the distance, her mind blank. Her heartbeat slowed as she pushed the swing. Back and forth, back and forth. She prayed out loud, "I want you to find Rosie—please, God." She took a deep breath and held it for a moment to force the oxygen into her brain. She rubbed her eyes and whispered, "Lord, help them finish grilling me and help us find Rosie before anyone hurts her. Please."

She walked back to the cottage and paused when a dove cooed. A faint smile tugged at her lips. Perhaps God had sent her a message in the peaceful coo of the dove.

After two hours of non-stop interrogation, the Door County officers left the cottage, instructing her to stay in the county.

Chief Maxwell shut the door behind them and turned to Piper. "Brutal questioning. You okay?"

Piper nodded. "Do they believe I did it?"

"Hard to say, but they asked the same questions I would have asked."

"Do you think I did it?"

"No. I know you didn't hurt Rosie and you wouldn't hurt anyone else. You're too sweet."

Piper blushed and turned away from his stare. "I need something comfortable to wear. Will the police let you pick up my things from the camper?"

"No. That's off limits, and I won't even ask. What's your size? I'll run into Sister Bay. I saw some shops along the main road. What do you want? Sweats?"

She waved a hand. "I don't care. No one's going to see me anyway."

Chief Maxwell rested his hand on his heart and gasped. "Glad to hear I'm 'no one.'"

Piper rolled her eyes. "Spare me. You don't count. You're the police."

His eyes clouded and he turned away to clear his throat. "I'll drive into town to see what's open. There's fresh coffee in the kitchen." He stopped at the door and said, "I wouldn't bank on no one seeing how you're dressed today."

"What do you mean?"

He stepped back from the door as Dominique Landry pushed past him, her arms out. "Baby, come here." She reached for Piper and pulled her into a tight hug.

"Mrs. Landry? What are you doing here?" Piper swallowed over the lump in her throat.

"When Chief Maxwell said Rosie was in trouble, we all dropped everything. I'm here to cook for everyone. Robby wants to join the search party to find Rosie. Your parents and Rosie's brothers are on the way. Ruby packed her fancy portable coffee machine to keep you in lattes. We're going to fix everything, baby."

Piper leaned into Dominque and breathed in the yeasty smell of rolls and bread. The lump in her throat grew until tears rolled down her cheeks.

"That's okay, baby. You cry those tears. This is terrible." She turned to Chief Maxwell. "Do *not* tell me the police suspect my baby girl?"

"I can't say right now."

"Well, Chief Maxwell. They need to leave Piper alone." Dominique pulled Piper close to her chest and hummed a tune in her ear as she rocked Piper.

The door clicked shut and Dominique stepped away from Piper, smoothing her hand across Piper's flyaway hair. "Let's get you something for your eyes. If your mama and daddy show up seeing those puffy eyes, they'll worry." She pulled Piper into the kitchen and handed her a cool cloth. "You go sit and rest. I'll whip up something to eat."

Piper laid her hand on her stomach and groaned. "I can't eat a bite, Dominique."

"Shh. Don't tell me what you can't do right now. This house is about to fill up with Cranberry Harbor folks who love you and Rosie, and I will not let them go hungry. If you want to starve yourself, that's up to you, but my folks need to eat." She pointed to the couch. "Go. Take it easy."

The doorbell rang as people who loved Piper and Rosie came to help. Piper's parents arrived before lunch and breezed into the cottage. Her mother glanced around and smiled. "I'm so glad you found a decent place to stay. I worried about you sleeping in that camper, and considering what's happened, it appears I was correct. Glamping was a disaster." She pulled Piper into a hug. "I'm so sorry, sweetheart. How are you? Why are you still wearing your evening dress?"

Piper grimaced. "Well, Mom, between running from a murder scene, worrying about my best friend, and being grilled by the local police, I ran out of time to change my clothes."

Piper's dad sat on the other side of her, patting her hand. "We will figure this out."

Piper pulled her hand away from her dad before she snapped at his constant patting. "I don't know how, Daddy."

He nodded.

The doorbell rang again, and Ruby breezed in with a colossal coffee pot. "I can't fix this, but I can keep my friend full of caffeine.

Hello, Sarah. Jack." She blew a kiss across the room to Piper and hurried into the kitchen.

Piper leaned against her dad's shoulder and drifted off to sleep.

When Piper woke from her rest, the cottage was a miniature recreation of downtown Cranberry Harbor. A plate of sandwiches waited on the table. Something in the oven filled the house with the scent of chocolate, and Dominique issued orders like a drill sergeant. Ruby brewed lattes and kept everyone's cups full of caffeine. Sarah Haydn sat in the corner, knitting and tapping her toes on the plush carpet.

Her father helped steady her as she sat up and rubbed her eyes. "Sleep well?"

Piper groaned. "My body feels like I got run over by a truck."

Jack Haydn's eyes darkened. "I'm sorry you're dealing with this again, honey."

"I know, Daddy. We need to find Rosie." The lump in her throat ached. She was tired of choking back tears.

"We'll find her. Rosie's brother Kennedy came. Your brother Chase, Robby, and several others from town will join the search team."

Piper nodded. "I can't stop worrying. What if she's hurt or . . ." A sob escaped her throat and Jack Haydn pulled her into his arms.

"Come on, sweetheart. Have faith."

She nodded against his sweater. "I'm trying, Dad, but this is so hard."

Chief Maxwell pushed through the crowd milling in the front room of the cottage carrying a bright orange bag. His eyes searched the room, and he nodded when he saw Piper. He held the bag up high over the crowd.

Piper pushed through the room and reached for the bag. "Thank you," she whispered. "How much do I owe you?"

He waved his hand. "We'll settle up later. I'm heading to the park if you want to ride with me."

Piper's eyes searched his. "Did you hear anything?"

He mouthed the word *no* and stepped back. "I'd like to leave as soon as possible."

Piper nodded and hurried upstairs to a quiet room to change. She laid out the jeans and pumpkin-orange sweatshirt and unwrapped a moss-green scarf that perfectly complemented the top. She slipped out of the formal dress and breathed a sigh of relief, then ran a brush through her hair and tied the scarf around her neck.

Piper ran down the stairs and clamped her lips closed. She had almost yelled out that she was ready but stopped short. The living room and kitchen had turned into an impromptu prayer meeting. Dominique knelt in the kitchen doorway, and Piper's parents knelt at the couch. Chief Maxwell stood near the door, his hands held in the air and his head bowed. Their lips murmured as they followed Robby's prayer.

"Dear Jesus, we beg you to find our friend Rosie and return her to us unharmed. We ask you to foil the plans of the evil one and work your mighty life-giving power in Rosie's favor. Please, God—let the searchers find her and help us trust while we wait."

"Yes, Lord . . ." echoed around the room. Tears sprung to Piper's eyes, and a weight lifted from her chest.

"Yes, Lord. Help me trust," she whispered. She wiped her eyes and stepped through the crowd toward the chief.

The front door opened, and a petite woman stood at the door, glaring. "What is going on here?" She glanced around the room until her eyes rested on Piper. She pointed. "Are you Piper?"

Piper gulped and stammered. "Yes, ma'am."

"Did you rent the cottage for one person or . . ." She trailed off and searched the room. "Twenty people? The agreement is explicit. This"—she waved her hands—"I can't allow."

Will stepped near the woman and pulled out his badge. "My apologies. We are here forming a search party for our friend who's missing from the state park. My friend Piper here has quite a support team, and we didn't take time to alert you."

The woman rested her hand on her chest. "Oh, my! How can we help?"

"Can we use your cottage for our base? I'll pay extra," Jack Haydn asked.

"Of course. Of course. Don't worry about it. We will settle when you find your missing friend." She glared at Chief Maxwell. "Why haven't I heard anything about this on the news?"

"I'm not privy to the investigation. I'm here to search for our friend."

"Whatever you need. Let us know." She backed out of the front door and hurried across the lawn.

"I'm heading to the park. Who's riding with me?" Will called.

Piper and Robby followed him to the car in silence. Nothing mattered but finding Rosie.

Rosie trembled against a rough plank pressing into her cheek. She wiggled her numb fingers and her frozen feet. Her eyelids weighed a thousand pounds. She attempted to adjust her position, but moving was impossible.

C# leaned on the post across from Rosie, her hands and feet tied with white ropes.

"Carolyn, why are you tied up?" Rosie's throat burned. When they dumped her here and tied her up last night, Carolyn had been the one to tie Rosie's wrists behind her back.

Carolyn grimaced. "I don't know."

"Weren't you part of this tying-me-up business?"

"No. I never wanted to hurt you. Piper, though . . ."

"Don't say anything mean about Piper," Rosie said. "How are we going to get out of here?"

"I don't think we will." She tugged at her ropes. "He tied me pretty tight."

"He who?"

"My brother."

Rosie's eyes widened. "Your brother?"

C# leaned her head on the wood rail and closed her eyes.

"Are we still in the park?"

"Yes, we're on top of the Eagle Tower. Don't you recognize it?"

"Nope," Rosie said. "I've never been here before this week. Someone should find us soon if we're still in the park. What about your husband? Won't he miss you?"

Carolyn snorted. "He's not my husband, and I don't think he misses me."

"What do you mean?"

"Forget about it."

Rosie's eyes narrowed. "What's going on, Carolyn Sharpe?"

"Just shut up, Rosie. The less you know the better."

Robby and Piper followed Chief Maxwell to his police car.

Dominique ran behind them. "Wait up! You forgot the sandwiches!" She pressed a bag into her husband's hand and took his face in her hands. "You find my Rosie Baby, Robby. Hear me?" she whispered.

Robby nodded and reached for his wife's cheek. He rubbed his hand on her skin and smiled. "Yes, ma'am. We'll bring Rosie home."

"Alive," she said. "Please."

Piper gulped and slipped into the backseat of the police car. The hard plastic seat and the grid between her and the front seat sent a shiver up her spine. She had never seen the backseat of a police car before. *Please, God—never let me ride back here as a criminal.* She fiddled with the soft yarn fringe at the edge of the scarf, her fingers moving between the strands, twisting and combing out the yarn. Today the beautiful scenery of Door County hid behind eerie fog and cold, gray skies.

"The search team is well underway," Chief Maxwell said. His eyes found hers in his rearview mirror. He nodded. "We'll find her."

Piper swallowed over the lump in her throat and glanced away.

"You bet we'll find her, Miss Piper. No worrying now," Robby said. "The good Lord's got your friend Rosie in the palm of his hand. No worrying now. I'm sorry to say, Miss Piper, but I can't help but think that whenever they spend a little time with Rosie, they'll bring her back. She's a handful, that one."

Piper grinned. "I wish that were true, Robby."

"Like I said, honey—no worrying."

Piper nodded and bit her tongue to stop the tears pooling in the corner of her eyes.

"Half of Cranberry Harbor is at the park searching for Rosie, Miss Piper."

She smiled. "The other half is back at the Airbnb cooking food."

Chief Maxwell smiled in the mirror. "That's one thing I've noticed in my tenure at Cranberry Harbor. Your town adores good food."

Robby smiled. "Yes, sir. And my wife is bossing everyone around." He held up the bag of sandwiches. "Probably enough sandwiches here for the whole search team."

"Dominique is a very special lady, Robby," Piper said.

"That she is, and so are you, Miss Piper. And so is Rosie. The Lord knows. He knows, Piper. Hold on."

Piper nodded and stopped fighting the lump in her throat. Tears ran down her cheek and she whispered the words in her heart: "Please, God—save my friend."

The Door County Sheriff's Department had set up a staging area near the middle of the park—far from their campsite. Piper wanted to poke around their site in the daylight and see what she had missed, but Chief Maxwell had already warned her the camper was off limits.

Piper followed the men to the middle of the crowded area.

Robby held up Dominique's bag. "Sandwiches over here." The crowd surrounded the table, grabbing the food and mumbling their thanks.

"Who did you bring?" an officer asked Chief Maxwell.

He pointed to Robby and Piper and spelled their names as the officer wrote on a clipboard. He glanced up at Piper and pointed. "No going near your campsite. I'll hold you responsible if she's found there, Maxwell."

"Yes, sir." He nodded and took the map the officer held out.

"You three stay together. Find your area of the park and follow the map. Walk in a line and keep your eyes open—up, down, side to side. Take your time. We'd rather take longer to cover the park than hurry through and miss something. Got it?"

Chief Maxwell nodded and hurried back to the police car. "Faster if we drive to our area. Let's go."

Several minutes later the three found their section to search and began walking in a line. Piper huffed. "We aren't accomplishing anything here. We won't find her out in the open."

"Hey—this is all part of the process, and we hope to find clues too."

"Well, I'm searching for Rosie. You guys watch for everything else." She hurried ahead until Robby called out.

"Slow down, Miss Piper. We must do this right."

She blew out a breath and fell back in line. Her whispered prayer hammered in her heart. "Please, God—save my friend."

Piper walked with Robby and Chief Maxwell for miles before they turned back to the police car. Piper's legs burned, and her neck stiffened from looking up and down all afternoon. The sunset blazed orange and red behind the pine trees, but Piper ignored the beauty. Instead, as darkness gathered, her heart hammered and her mind raced. Someone must have found Rosie by now.

"Did you call again?" she asked Chief Maxwell.

"I'm sorry. No news."

"I want to scream." Piper clenched her fists to calm her racing heart.

"Maybe you should."

"Should what, Chief Maxwell?"

"Will."

"Huh?"

"You should call me Will, and yes, you should scream. We're out in the woods. Do you mind if the lady screams, Robby?"

Robby smiled. "No, sir. I don't mind anything Miss Piper does. When she was a young 'un, she sure bellowed when chasing after her brothers." He grinned. "I'm suspectin' grown-up Piper has some of that vinegar left in her that baby Piper had."

Piper grinned. "Thanks, Robby, but I'd feel stupid to let loose in front of you two, so I'll keep deep breathing and praying."

Robby squeezed Piper's shoulder and said, "That's all we can do, Piper. I'll add my prayers to yours, and something's gotta happen soon. I feel it."

"Chief Maxwell?"

"*Will.*"

"Will, do you think someone took her out of the park? If no one's found a clue all day, we're wasting our time here, aren't we?"

"The Sheriff said they have officers checking the airports in Green Bay, Appleton, and Milwaukee. They checked the passenger list for the ferry to Washington Island. So far nothing to report."

"She didn't vanish. Where are you, Rosie?" she yelled.

Her eyes met Will's, and she turned away at the sadness mirrored there.

"Come on," Will said. "Let's get back to the check-in station and catch up. Then I'm getting you back to the cottage to rest."

"I don't want to go back to the cottage." Piper stamped her foot and gritted her teeth.

"Well, Miss Haydn, you can't stay out here in the dark, and your father won't forgive me if I lose you out here. So the cottage is the only option."

Piper followed the men to the car, her hope for the safe return of her zany red-haired friend dimming by the second.

Rosie leaned against the wood. Her head throbbed, and she shivered. When she focused her eyes, the dim scene in front of her moved in and out. She squeezed her eyes and opened them again. Carolyn was gone. She pushed her feet against the floor and attempted to sit up straighter.

"How did Carolyn disappear?" She groaned. Her arms weighed her down. The pins and needles prickling up and down her muscles kept her from trying to untie her hands. Goosebumps rippled across her arms, and she shivered.

"All right, girl. Slow your breathing. Not a good time for a panic attack." The sky darkened and birds called in the trees above and around her. She swallowed a lump in her throat. "I'm spending another wonderful night tied up in the great outdoors." A tear trickled down her cheek. "Me and my bright ideas. No wonder Piper gets upset with me. Why did I insist on this trip and staying in Old Bess?" She closed her eyes and rested her throbbing head. "They'll find me in the morning," she mumbled and drifted to sleep.

CHAPTER 8

Monday

Piper's eyes popped open, and she checked her phone for texts. Nothing. She sat up and gingerly picked her way across the room. Dominique and Ruby lay on air mattresses on the floor. Piper's mother lay on the bed across the room. Wearing an eye mask and some expensive cream dabbed on her face, Sarah Haydn snored softly. Piper smiled. Her mother would vehemently deny that snoring, but Piper heard her plain as day.

Piper slipped into the robe on the back of the bedroom door and pulled the belt around her as she tiptoed down the steep staircase. The men slept on the couch and living room floor. She craved coffee but didn't know how to navigate the room without stepping on someone. She sat on the bottom step.

"Coffee, Miss Haydn?" Chief Maxwell stood in front of her with a steaming mug.

"Oh, thank you, Chief," she whispered.

"*Will*," he said.

"Will. I'll try. Sorry."

He sat on the floor at the end of the stairs. "Your brother Chase got in last night. He brought his drone."

"Oh, that's a good idea. Will they let him operate the drone in the park?"

"We will check this morning. You sleep okay?"

Piper sipped the hot liquid. "I did, but I can't stop worrying about Rosie."

"Me too." His brown eyes clouded. "Today's the day. I can feel it. We'll find her or we'll find a clue."

"A clue's not good enough," Piper whispered, and a tear rolled down her cheek. "What if we *never* find her?"

His hand covered hers and she glanced up, shocked at the jolt his touch caused. "Keep the faith, Piper. What would Rosie tell you right now?"

Piper closed her eyes for a moment and grinned. "She'd say, 'Piper Haydn, quit your sniveling and get your fanny out here to find me!'"

Will smiled. "See? You know what to do. I'm eager to get going, but it's too early. Let's let them sleep a little while longer and then we'll make some noise."

"I'm going to sleep for a week after this."

Will smiled. "I know you want to despair, but despair means you still believe in something. Some*one*."

"Shostakovich said that." She smiled. "Are you secretly a classical music fan, Chief Maxwell?"

Will smiled. "You never know, Miss Haydn." He tapped his phone and the soft strains of "The Gadfly Suite" played.

Piper closed her eyes and leaned her head on the wall while the notes filled her heart with peace.

"We'll find her, Piper. Keep the faith."

Rosie's head throbbed, and she shivered. "This isn't funny anymore. Where is everyone?" Her throat burned and her vision blurred. She blinked several times and opened her eyes, willing her brain to cooperate. "Where am I?" She glanced around the platform. The tops of trees peeked over the rail. "Wherever I am, it's not on the ground." Rosie groaned and leaned her head back. Carolyn had never come back.

A tear trickled down her cheek. Some called her Pollyanna. But this seemed impossible. *If only I'd kept my mouth shut when I heard that ruckus outside.*

She had been in the bunk in the pop-up roof, getting ready to read by flashlight. Maybe if she had stayed there, no one would have noticed her. *But no. Me and my big mouth.*

When she heard shouting, Rosie hopped down from the bunk and peeked through the camper windows, but they stood outside of her line of vision. The muffled voices kept her from hearing anything they said, but then the man fell into the fire pit and the woman turned. Rosie recognized C# and slammed open the camper door, yelling and flailing her arms and legs, acting as though she knew martial arts. When she kicked out, the man held her leg and jerked her to the ground. *Hence, the knot on the back of my head.*

Her dress snagged on the cupboard and ripped, leaving her top loose. *I liked this dress too.* Anger rose in her chest at the audacity of the strange man to ruin her vintage dress, much less bonk her head on the ground and tie her up somewhere in the wilderness. Fury surged through her body, warming her cold limbs.

If I ever get another chance to swing, I'm gonna make contact. She smiled and closed her eyes. *Someone will find me. I know they will. Right, Lord?*

Rosie whispered her favorite Bible verse—Isaiah 40:31: "But they that wait upon the Lord shall renew their strength; they shall mount up with wings as eagles; they shall run, and not be weary; and they shall walk, and not faint."

In the cottage, controlled chaos reigned. Dominique stood over a griddle, grilling breakfast sandwiches. Ruby brewed pots of coffee and filled thermoses. Sarah Haydn passed out sandwiches and refilled mugs with steaming hot coffee. Jack Haydn and Chief Maxwell sat at the dining table with Kennedy, Chase, and Robby. Piper stood next to her father, listening to their plans. They would check in with the local sheriff's department and clear Chase's drone usage and see what the officials planned for the day. After that, Chief Maxwell suggested they go back through the areas they searched yesterday one more time. "It can't hurt anything, and we might see something we missed."

Robby smiled and stood. "Gentlemen, I like your plans, but I believe we need to submit these to the dear Lord and follow his plans for our search. Okay?"

Nods around the table gave him the go-ahead, and his deep voice rumbled across the table. The clattering in the kitchen stopped, and the women stood in the doorway, their heads bowed. "Dear Father, we want to find our sweet friend Roosevelt Hale today. She's probably tired and afraid and cold and we are worried. Open our eyes to see what you'd have us to see. Open our hearts to your leading. Help us submit to the local authorities. But most of all, dear Lord, help us find our friend soon. Your Word says that when we wait on you, you'll renew our strength and help us fly high like the eagles without weariness or fainting. Help us be like the eagles and renew our strength."

Amens echoed around the cottage, and Piper wiped the tears from the corner of her eyes. Robby's prayer soothed her mind and reminded her to trust God in impossible times.

Will tapped his finger on the maps spread across the table.

"What?" Piper asked.

"The Eagle Tower in the park. Did anyone check there?" He frowned. "We'll ask the sheriff when we get to the park this morning."

"What's stopping us? Let's go." Piper said. A new clue energized her tired body and hope of finding her friend grew in her heart.

Will stood and jangled his keys. "Going with us, men?"

The men nodded and reached for breakfast sandwiches and their mugs.

"Bring my baby girl back today." Dominique stood in the kitchen doorway, staring at Will. "You hear me? No messing around. That little girl needs finding, and she needs it today. Get on with yourselves now and bring her home." She stood on her tiptoes and kissed Robby. "That goes for you too, mister."

Robby nodded and grinned. "Yes, ma'am."

The Door County sheriff and her officers milled around the table in the White Cedar Nature Center. Will squeezed into the crowd, unfazed by a gathering of police officers. Piper stood with Kennedy and watched while Will talked to the sheriff, then stepped closer to listen to the discussion.

"Did he file the permit for drone flight?" The sheriff stood with her hands on her hips, glaring at Will. "I can't help him. The DNR requires a two-week notice and an application. I can't change the law."

"Not even for a missing person?" Piper gasped.

The sheriff jabbed her finger in Piper's direction. "Listen—I want to find her too. I understand your frustration, but I can't change the rules. A personal drone won't see much in these trees anyway. He can fly it from the water but not the land. That's the best I can offer."

"Doesn't your office have a drone?" Will asked.

The sheriff pinched her lips together. "We do, but it needs repairs—got slammed into a tree last time we used it. We hope to get parts replaced after the new budget talks. Listen, Chief Maxwell—we are a small county of small towns, and we have limited funds."

"I understand," he said. "Did anyone check the top of the Eagle Tower?"

The sheriff clenched her jaw and rubbed a purple mark on her cheek. "No, it's closed for repairs too. Steps are out or something. Stay away from there."

"Eagle Tower is open!" a voice called from the back of the nature center.

The sheriff whirled around and glared at the clerk behind the counter. "What do you mean? I walked past the tower myself. There's a chain with a padlock pulled across the stairs."

The clerk held up a sheet. "The report this morning of areas closed, repairs, or park news does not state that the tower is closed."

Piper's eyes caught Will's glance, and he nodded toward his car. She ran to catch up to him as Robby and Chase piled into Will's police car. He started speeding down the road before Piper had fully closed the car door.

She rested her hand on her chest and gasped for breath. "Do you think she's there?"

"No idea, but we'll find out."

"Hold on, Miss Piper," Robby said. "This-here chief of police is going to be the death of us all." Robby gripped the door handle and raised his eyebrows. A small grin pulled at the corner of his lips. "Feels like I'm on one of those crime shows Dominique loves to watch. Oooh boy, Chief Will."

Chase gripped the bar behind Will's head, and his knuckles whitened. Piper whispered over and over, "Please, God—let her be there. Please, God."

"What did the sheriff say about my drone?" Chase asked.

"You need to launch it from a boat because you didn't fill out a permit two weeks ago."

Chase snorted. "Rosie wasn't missing two weeks ago."

Will nodded. "Rules don't always make sense."

Piper rested her hand on her brother's hand. "We'll find her." She smiled.

Chase ran his hand through his hair.

"When did you get so worried about Rosie?" Piper asked.

"I've always worried about Rosie," Chase replied. He coughed and glanced away. Piper considered his level of concern. Chase usually flew through life, taking the easy road, never missing an opportunity to party. Joining a search team and camping on the floor of a cottage wasn't his norm. *Maybe he's made that turnaround that Mom and Dad have prayed for.*

Will navigated the cruiser through the park, driving fast while avoiding pedestrians and bicycles like a pro. He stopped at the parking lot for the Eagle Tower, and they hurried out of the car.

A siren sounded on the road behind them and a Door County Sheriff's car pulled into the parking lot. The sheriff and another officer hopped out. "You ran out. We're trying to work together here." She eyed him with a long stare until Will nodded.

"I'm sorry. She's our friend. This one's personal," Will said.

"All the more reason you should let us do our job."

"Yes, ma'am," Will said.

"Let's go," the sheriff said, and they followed her to the stairs of the Eagle Tower. Piper held her breath. If they didn't find a clue or Rosie, she didn't know what she would do. Despair threatened to envelop her. She didn't have the energy to fight anymore.

A sign hung from the chain padlocked across the stairs. "Closed for stair repair."

"Who hung that if it's not officially from the park?" Robby asked.

The sheriff held up the bolt cutters she had carried from the car and snipped through the chain. She turned to the group from Cranberry Harbor. "Be my guest." She pointed up the stairs. Chase and Kennedy sprinted past her, with Robby, Chief Maxwell, and Piper close behind.

Piper climbed slowly, her eyes scanning across each step. She whispered the only prayer she could muster: "God, please help us. Help us find Rosie."

Piper scanned the stairs as she climbed. A flicker of purple fluttered on a step above her and she hurried to investigate reaching out to grab the fabric.

"Stop!" Chief Maxwell called.

Piper pulled her hand back as if someone had slapped her. Her cheeks burned when she turned to Chief Maxwell.

"Let the officer pick it up," he ordered.

"It's from Rosie's dress." A sob rose in her throat. "The one she wore that day."

"Okay, this is good. Stand there and wait for the officer and do not touch anything. Not even the handrail." He hurried up the steps, leaving Piper to wait by the fabric.

She glanced through the trees out to the lake, and a chill ran down her spine. "What time I am afraid I will trust in thee," she whispered. *What's taking so long?* She jumped at a shout above. *Is that Chase?* Footsteps rumbled down the stairs above her and she glanced up.

Chase burst around the corner, yelling, "We found a shoe and hair!"

Piper's stomach lurched. "Rosie's hair?"

Chase nodded. "Yes—red, curly."

"Oh, Chase." A sob escaped, and Chase wrapped his arms around her.

"Keep the faith, Pip. She's out there."

Piper nodded against her brother's chest, and a tear trickled down her cheek. "Whenever we find her, I'm going to yell at her for scaring us like this."

"Exactly," Chase said and pulled Piper close, resting his chin on her head.

Chief Maxwell and the Door County Sheriff came down to the step where Piper waited by Rosie's fabric. The sheriff slipped on a glove and collected the fabric, slipping the torn piece into a bag. She held out the bag with hair fibers. "Any chance this is your friend's hair?"

Piper gulped at the long, red, curly strands. "Yes."

"We found the hair on a nail at the top. Appears, they tied her there for a while. Other than this shoe, we didn't find anything." She held out a pink patent leather stiletto. "Is this familiar?"

"That's not Rosie's," Piper said. "But I know who that belongs to. C#."

"Excuse me?"

"C#. She's married to the ranger that kept ticketing us."

The sheriff groaned. "All right. Let's get back to the nature center. I'll catalog this and check on the search team's plans."

Piper glanced out at the lake. "What if someone took her out of the park by crossing the lake? It's close enough."

"I'll call and get someone to search the waterfront," she said, holding up the evidence. "Let's get back to the center and check in with the search team."

Piper stood in the clearing at the base of the eagle tower with her eyes closed and a hand on her chest. She listened to the water and the wind rustling through the trees above. She opened her eyes and turned in a circle, staring straight ahead, searching for clues. Nothing caught her eye, and she slumped, disappointed. After they found Rosie, she would never leave Cranberry Harbor again. *I'll become a hermit. No more adventures for me. I've had enough for one lifetime.*

They joined the search team gathered back at the nature center. A Door County officer turned to Piper. "Who's this 'C Sharpe'?"

Piper explained their history and what she knew of her after the conference. "But that's all I know. We haven't kept in touch. She said she's married to the park ranger, but I never saw them together. I haven't seen her since the other night at the conference when she disappeared before she won her award."

The sheriff pulled up behind the knot of gathered searchers. "DNR called. The victim is not a park ranger," she said when she approached their group.

Piper's head spun, and she plopped down on the park bench. The sheriff sat across from her. "Why did that information affect you so much?"

"He wrote us tickets and cited all the rules we broke. He drove that golf cart and wore a uniform. C# said he was a ranger. I never believed he was a fake. Why would he impersonate a park ranger?"

"We don't know. I have officers searching for information."

Piper rubbed her eyes and considered each interaction. "He didn't write tickets to other campsites. At least not that I noticed."

"Why do you think he fixated on you?"

"I don't know. He knew we knew his wife when we were kids."

The sheriff turned to Chief Maxwell, and the others gathered around. "We're calling off the search at five tonight."

"No!" Piper yelled. "What if she's out there with some evil person?"

The sheriff held up her hand. "We will continue to investigate and follow leads, but I can't keep my officers at the park when we have an entire county to protect."

Tears rolled down Piper's cheeks. Chase wrapped his arms around her. "We'll never stop, Piper. We'll find her."

Piper nodded against his jacket, but her hope from earlier in the day dissipated. She didn't know what to think. Her friend didn't just disappear. She was out there waiting for them to find her.

"Kennedy and Robby are doubling back to search their area again. Let's you and I walk down to the water," Chase said. "See what we can see. Keep your eyes on the trail."

"For breadcrumbs?"

"Something like that," Chase said.

The wind rustled through the pines, and Chase followed Piper to the lake. They watched the path, checking for signs of Rosie.

At the water's edge Piper scanned the horizon. "How far is it to Michigan? They might have her anywhere, Chase."

"Fifty miles, I think. But let's not think about that. I have to believe we'll find her." He squeezed Piper's shoulders and surveyed the beach. "Let's walk a little and keep our eyes open."

The cool wind combined with her wet shoes chilled Piper, but she refused to quit. She and Chase walked as far along the rocky beach as possible. When the cliffs jutted into the bay, blocking their path, they turned around to find the search group.

Piper turned to the beach with her hands on her hips. "I'm going to walk slower and scan every inch of this beach. I know it's foolish with all the miles of beaches in Door County and all that open water, but this is next to the Eagle Tower where we found a piece of her dress. What if she's out here somewhere."

"Did someone have a boat waiting? Are they throwing us off track by making us think they left this way?" Chase rubbed the back of his neck and scanned the beach. "Where else should we look? What are we missing?"

Piper walked up the beach away from the water's edge. She stood in one spot and turned in a slow circle, scanning as she moved. Then she took several steps forward and turned in a circle again.

"What are you doing, Pip?" Chase stepped behind her.

"I'm making sure I search everything before we walk away from here. I have a feeling we'll find a clue on this beach, but I don't know. Why don't you jog to the other end, where the cliff comes out, and work your way back? Scan the rocks, the trees, everything on the beach. We'll meet in the middle."

Chase jogged down the beach, and Piper returned to her scanning. She moved down the beach slowly, her eyes cataloging everything in front of her. Sticks and trash. Leftover wood from a fire and old beer cans. Nothing seemed disturbed. Nothing seemed out of the ordinary. *Time to give up, Piper. She's gone.*

Her heart pounded in her chest and a roar ripped open her throat. "Rosie, where are you?" Piper yelled. Her voice echoed on the rocks. Chase ran up to her, eyes wide.

"What happened? Did you see her?"

"No." Piper wiped a tear from her eye. "I'm frustrated, and I yelled for Rosie."

"Come with me and tell me what you think," Chase said, reaching for Piper's hand.

He ran down the beach, and Piper struggled to keep his pace. Her foot slipped on the wet rocks several times and the wind sucked the breath from her lungs. She stopped to rest and gulp air. She leaned over and rested her hands on her knees as her chest heaved.

Chase turned back and grinned. "When's the last time you hit the gym, Pip?"

Piper sucked in a deep breath and turned to her brother with narrowed eyes. "Shut up, Chase Haydn."

He reached for her hand. "Come on—I don't know if I found anything, but I want you to see. If I can find a boat to rent, I'll fly the drone over this beach first. What do you think?"

"Let's go." Piper followed her brother, stumbling across the rocks and gasping for air.

Chase pulled her along the beach several feet and pointed to a pile of brush underneath a rocky overhang. "Should we check in there? Seems like a good place to hide something."

Piper glanced around the area. "Nothing seems touched in here for years. Do you see footprints?"

"No, I'm sure the rocks hide any prints, but let's drag the brush out and check. We won't have to worry that we didn't investigate. Something about this area kept pulling me back, but I wanted you with me."

Piper scrambled up the incline and held onto the rock above her head while she stepped down into the space. Brush lay stacked in the center and trash surrounded the sticks and rocks. She leaned into the space, letting her eyes adjust to the dim light. A smooth piece of wood caught her eye, and she leaned closer—forgetting that she stood on wet rocks. Her shoe slid, and she pitched face-first into the brush.

"Piper!" Chase yelled.

Piper pushed away from the brush pile. "I'm okay, but you're right. The brush is covering something. Give me a hand."

Chase yanked at the brush, and Piper followed. The branches scratched her hands, but she didn't care. They had to find Rosie. She would baby her piano hands after her friend came home. The water lapped at the rocky beach. Birds called overhead, Chase huffed and puffed, and she grunted every time she threw a branch outside the cave-like space.

"It's a rowboat," Chase said. "Upside down. Help me."

Piper scrambled around the pile to stand next to her brother. Under the brush a white wooden boat lay upside down in the sand. She nudged it with her foot. "It's heavy. Do you think we can lift it?" Chase pushed up his shirt sleeves. "I'm going to try." He leaned into the boat's edge and reached underneath to grab a corner. "Ugh. The sand is around the base. We need a shovel."

Piper moved another pile of brush and froze.

"What? Why are you standing there like that? What's wrong?" Chase ran back to Piper.

The color drained from her face, and she pointed. Chase followed her finger and dropped to the ground, shoving his shoulder against the boat.

A ruffle of colorful fabric spread across the sand and disappeared underneath the boat.

"Rosie," Piper wailed. "Rosie, hang on. We're here. We're here. Hold on. Please."

Piper frantically scooped sand and rocks from the edge of the boat while Chase shoved the heavy wood. They only needed an inch for Chase to reach underneath and lift the boat.

"Help!" Piper yelled.

Chase grunted. "They'll never hear us out here. Can you call?"

Piper dropped to the rocky sand and pulled her phone from her pocket. Her finger shook as she punched in Will's number. When he answered the phone, Piper shouted. "Will, we think we found something. Rosie's dress. But we need help." She gasped for breath and tried to focus on his voice.

"Where are we? Straight down from the Eagle Tower on the beach. We turned to the left. The left, Chase?"

Chase nodded.

"Yes, the left. Hurry!"

Chase braced his feet against the rock and shoved the boat. Sweat rolled down his red face and his cheeks puffed with the exertion. Piper scooped sand and grimaced as rock spiders skittered across her fingers.

"Chase, you can get your hands under here." She scrambled out of his way and he rushed to her spot. His hands fit into the groove Piper had dug, and he reached in and pushed. The boat lifted and Piper screamed.

On the beach lay Rosie, a dark red stain across her torn dress. Her matted hair and swollen lips drew attention from the odd angle of her neck.

Piper slid down onto the sand next to her friend. Tears poured down her cheeks. "Oh, Rosie. Roosevelt Hale. Please be alive. Please. Oh, Chase."

Chase wiped tears from his eyes and glanced out at the beach. "Should I pick her up and run?"

"Don't move her. She's okay, right? She's going to live, right? Chase? Chase!"

Chase wiped tears from his eyes. "Can you check her pulse?"

Piper leaned over Rosie and reached for her wrist. "I don't know. I'm not sure. Run out and see how close Will is. Maybe you should grab her." She patted Rosie's cheek. "Listen to me, Roosevelt Hale—if you die on me, I'll never forgive you. Come on. I need you. We all need you. Hold on. Just hold on, Rosie—please."

Chase ducked his head under the limestone overhang. "They're almost here."

"Tell someone to run back for a stretcher and call 9-1-1."

Chase ran toward the rescuers, and Piper kept up her lecture to Rosie. "You haven't finished painting the preschool rooms at the academy. My parlor is a big mess from that wallpaper job. You have a lot of unfinished business. Come on, Rosie."

She held Rosie's cool fingers and rubbed them between her hands. *Dear God, please let her live. I need her.*

Shouting interrupted her prayer, and she jumped up and ran to the beach. "Hurry! She's in here!"

Will ran into the space under the rocky overhang, followed by the Door County officers.

Chase followed and wrapped his arms around Piper. "They called for an ambulance. Hold on. They're going to save her." His tears dropped into her hair and her tears rolled onto his shirt.

She leaned into her brother, praying the only words in her desperate heart: "Oh, God. Please help."

CHAPTER 9

Monday Afternoon

Piper watched the paramedics try to save Rosie, thankful for their presence, but white fiery anger bubbled inside. *How dare someone hurt my friend?* The sight of Rosie's waxy yellow skin twisted Piper's stomach. "Oh, please, God. Let her live," Piper whispered.

Chase stood behind her, patting her back. She stepped away from his hand. "Chase, you're jiggling my brain with all that thumping."

"Sorry, Pip," Chase said. His pale face and wide eyes softened Piper's annoyance, and she held his hand.

"Rosie will survive. She has to."

Chase nodded and swallowed, but his eyes gave away his doubts.

A whirring buzz overhead interrupted her worries. A helicopter landed inside the park. Piper watched as paramedics slid down the hill onto the beach and ran toward the rocky overhang. Her stomach twisted again, and she leaned into her brother. His hand steadied her. "Is it that bad, Chase? She needs a helicopter?"

"I don't know. I don't know."

Within minutes the paramedics whisked Rosie to the helicopter, and the machine rose and flew away. The noise of the blades echoed in Piper's ears. "Where are they taking her?"

"The trauma center in Madison," Will said.

"Can we go?" Chase asked.

"No," Will said. "Sorry. You two found her. They have questions. I'm going to drive her brother to the hospital. Sorry to leave you like this."

Piper gave into the anger swirling inside her and yelled. "They can wait! Rosie needs me!"

"Come on, Piper," Will said. "You know how this works. You're not free to leave until they talk to you. Rosie's in excellent hands right now. If they don't catch the killer, I don't think you two are safe."

A chill gripped Piper. "You don't think we're safe?"

"I don't know. They were at your campsite. What did they want? Why did they kill?"

Piper glanced out at the calm blue lake. Several officers combed the beach, searching for clues in the rocks and sand, while other officers investigated under the boat and the limestone overhang. Piper rubbed her eyes and shivered as a chill passed through her.

Piper sat across the table from the sheriff, twisting a paper napkin in her shaking hands. She took a deep breath and forced her spine straight. She would answer this woman's questions and get on the road to sit at the hospital with Rosie.

The woman flipped through pages in a file and rubbed a bruise on her cheek. Piper held back a sharp comment about the sheriff's lack of urgency. She glanced at the clock and adjusted her scarf. She jiggled her leg and closed her eyes. Impatience wouldn't hurry the sheriff, and Piper didn't want to risk annoying the woman. She waited with her eyes closed until sleep pulled at the corner of her mind and her head bobbed.

"Miss Haydn," the sheriff slammed the file closed and Piper jumped.

"Yes, ma'am."

"Here's why I'm concerned. You were involved in a murder last year and now you're my problem. Another murder in your vicinity and yet you appear squeaky clean. I don't believe for one second that you're not involved."

Piper's eyes widened and she spluttered. "But I was at a concert. She's my friend. I don't even own a gun."

The sheriff's eyes narrowed. "We will test for residue." She scribbled on the notepad and dropped the pen. "You made no secret that you didn't want to stay in the camper."

"So I shot my friend?" Piper's voice shot up two octaves and came out in a squeal.

"I don't know yet what you did, but trust me—I'll figure it out. Your daddy's money won't keep you out of trouble on this one. And neither will your relationship with Chief Maxwell. Got it?"

Piper nodded.

"Where were you at 8 p.m. Saturday night?"

"I was at the concert at the piano teachers conference. I told you this already."

"How did you get back to the campground?"

"I rode with a group staying at the park."

"I'll need their names." The sheriff shoved the notepad across the table and tossed Piper a pen.

"I need my phone to find the information," she said. "I didn't memorize anything."

"Write their names. I'll find them later. So you got back to the park and—"

"I told you. Our campsite was dark, and I turned on my phone flashlight so I wouldn't trip. I found the leg sticking out of the campfire and the pile of dirt. I didn't find Rosie, but I found her trashed glamper."

"Glamper?" The sheriff stared at her. "What's that?"

"Rosie called her camper a 'glamper' because she fixed it up pretty. You knew about Glamper Fest at the park?"

The sheriff nodded.

"Maybe one of them is jealous of her camper and did something to her." Piper pinched her nose between her eyes. "No. They all have their own cool campers. I don't know."

"You shot her. You didn't want to come with her—that's well documented. She's a bright personality. Maybe you're tired of competing with her? She's getting in your way and you removed her permanently?"

"No!" Piper yelled. "She's my friend. I don't want anything to happen to her."

"I'm not sure what I think about you finding her when my officers had already scoured that beach. Seems odd that you waltzed right to the exact hiding spot."

Piper dropped her eyes from the sheriff's intense gaze. She had nothing to hide and knew she was innocent, but the sheriff's stare scared her and her hands trembled. When she glanced up, the sheriff stared at her shaky hands and scribbled something on her notepad. Piper clenched her fist and dropped them into her lap as a bead of sweat rolled down her forehead.

"Wait—I didn't find her. My brother did."

The sheriff's eyebrows rose and she scribbled across the notepad. When she dropped the pen, she sat back in the chair and nodded her head. "Your brother. Hmmm . . . now that's even more interesting than *you* finding her. What's he doing up here anyway? Was he at Glamper Fest or the piano teachers conference?"

"No, he came when he heard about Rosie."

"Last time you were in trouble, wasn't he part of the situation?"

Piper gulped and nodded.

"So he shows up here for no good reason and magically finds our missing person. I'm not buying your story, Miss Haydn. You had enough time to concoct an alibi between you and your brother."

Piper twisted her fingers in her lap. A knock at the door jerked her attention away from her misery. A pale-faced deputy stuck his head through the door. "Her lawyer's here."

Piper's heart sank. *He's going to yell at me for talking, but why? I'm innocent.*

The sheriff stared at Piper. "You want to speak to him, or can we finish here?"

"We can finish," Piper whispered.

The sheriff stood and paced. "I'm fairly positive you and Chase are involved in this, and I'm going to scrutinize every area of your life. I hope you understand that your wealth won't help you here. Not in my county."

Piper nodded. "Yes, ma'am." She cleared her throat. "Did your officers search that island you can see from the beach? Horseshoe Island?"

The sheriff turned and stared at Piper with clenched teeth. "Miss Haydn, you aren't assuming you can do my job better than I can. Are you?"

"No, ma'am."

"Good. We're done. Sign your statement on this line, unless you want to talk to your attorney first. You'll wait in a cell until I'm done questioning you."

Piper reached for the paper and said, "I'll sign." Fear gnawed at Piper's belly as she scribbled her name, and her thoughts scattered. *A cell? I can't do a cell. Who else will be in there?*

A shiver ran down her spine and she bit the inside of her cheek to stop the tears stinging her eyes.

Lenny hurried in and shut the door. He dropped his briefcase onto the table and plopped into the chair across from Piper. "Why did you talk to her? The number-one rule is—"

"I know. 'Wait for Lenny.' But I didn't do anything, Lenny. I wanted her to believe me."

Lenny blew out a breath and skimmed Piper's statement. He squeezed the bridge of his nose and rubbed his eyes. "Your dad is going to fire me, Piper. I don't know if I can fix this." He dropped the paper onto the table and inhaled. "I need to see what mess Chase got himself into. No more talking—do you understand? Nothing. I'll get you out of here as soon as I can. You might have to wait a couple of hours."

Piper's belly clenched. "Okay," she whispered. "I'm sorry, Lenny."

Lenny waved and stuffed her statement into his briefcase. "Too late to be sorry. Don't complicate my job again."

Piper leaned her hands on the chair and startled when the cold metal touched her skin. *Well, God. I made a mess. Help. And please help me shut my mouth.*

Lenny held the door open for Piper and Chase. They huddled outside of the sheriff's department after he posted their bond. "The sheriff said you two have to stay in Door County until she's done with you. Do not leave. She also issued a warning that if she caught you snooping around her crime scene, she'd lock you up again. Got it?" He glanced at them over his eyeglasses.

Chase nodded, and Lenny patted him on the shoulder. "And you, Piper?"

"I can't go to the hospital to sit with Rosie?"

Lenny raised his eyebrows. "Staying in Door County means staying. Someone can send you updates. Chief Maxwell sent a text a few minutes ago. She's still in surgery."

Piper twisted the end of her scarf and chewed on her lip.

"Piper, I don't like the look on your face," Lenny said.

"Don't worry—I'll keep her out of trouble," Chase said.

Lenny cleared his throat. "That's exactly what worries me. You two are staying at the cottage? Everyone else left to get home, or they went to Madison to sit with Rosie."

Piper nodded.

"Good. I'll drop you off. I need to get back to Cranberry Harbor and catch up with your dad."

They followed Lenny to his car. Chase squeezed Piper's shoulder. "No one stayed behind at the cottage?"

"I don't know, but I need to close my eyes for a bit. I can't believe that woman let me sit in a jail cell for two hours." Piper shivered and her lip curled. "I need a shower."

Chase laughed. "You get used to it."

"That, my dear brother, is why you and I are not on the same wavelength. I will never get used to sitting in a jail cell."

Chase's Tesla sat alone in the cottage's driveway. "According to my texts, everyone abandoned us to sit with Rosie," he said.

"Probably for the better. We need to decompress and figure out how to get out of murder charges so I can go to her."

Chase groaned.

"What?"

"Nothing."

Piper tilted her head and stared at her brother, then pushed past him and punched the code into the door lock. "Lock that behind you. I don't want anyone surprising us." She plopped onto the leather sofa and gathered the fuzzy blanket around her shoulders. Her eyes closed and sleep called to her weary heart.

"What's this?"

Piper opened one eye and glanced at Chase. She flopped her head back onto the sofa and closed her eyes. "My notebook."

"I see that. What's it for?"

Piper yawned and sat up. "Rosie and I kept track of clues the last time we tried to solve a mystery, so I scribbled a few things about the odd happenings at the campground. Nothing too exciting in there. It's supposed to help solve the mystery, but I guess Rosie was the detective. I can't untangle anything."

Chase flipped through the pages. "Where's your notes on me from last time?"

Piper jumped from the sofa and snatched the paper from his hands. "Wrong notebook. But you, Chase Haydn, were a complete surprise. Nothing's written about you because I didn't suspect my own brother." She stared down her nose.

He held his hands in the air. "Hey—those days are past. I promise. I've turned over a new leaf."

She nudged him with her foot. "You better have. None of us can take your surprises anymore. Got it?"

He gave her a thumbs-up. "You got it, boss."

"I'm not kidding."

"I know, okay? Good grief."

"You act like you didn't give your entire family a heart attack every six months for the past five years."

Chase's cheeks reddened. "I'm sorry. I've made a lot of bad choices, but I'm trying to do better."

"I'm praying for you. I love you, man." She leaned over and hugged her brother.

He stretched his legs onto the coffee table. "Are you thinking what I'm thinking?"

Piper stood with her hands on her hips. "Rent a boat, fly your drone, and explore Horseshoe Island?"

"Exactly. She said stay in the county and we are."

"Well, she also told us to stay out of the investigation."

"We have to find out who did this to Rosie. If anything happens to . . ." Chase cleared his throat.

"Are you crying?" She leaned over and stared into his eyes. "You *are* crying. What's going on?" She gasped. "You have a crush on Rosie!"

Chase's face crumpled, and he hid behind his hands.

Piper dropped onto the sofa next to him and hugged her brother. "You big lug. I never guessed. How long has this been going on?"

"Since the first time you brought her home from school and she punched me in the nose for making fun of you," Chase whispered.

"Does she know?"

"Nah," he said. "I'm the big goof-up everyone tolerates. I'm not good enough for her."

Piper nudged his shoulder. "Get it together then, Chase."

"I'm trying. I swear I haven't done anything to get into trouble lately. No pot. No speeding. No helping crooks. Nothing."

"That's a good place to begin. You know Rosie wants a guy who loves God as much as she does."

Chase nodded, and a tear dripped down his cheek. "Maybe I can pray for her?"

Piper smiled. "Excellent. Now call and rent that boat. I'm going to close my eyes for a few minutes, but let me know when you're ready."

Chase nudged Piper. "I got the boat rented for twenty-four hours. Are you sure you don't want to wait until the morning? It might get dark soon."

"I want this investigation over so I can see Rosie. Let's go." Piper glanced at her phone. "No updates?"

"I didn't see anything."

Piper scrolled through her messages until she found Chief Maxwell's number.

---Any news?

---Still in surgery

---Ok. Let me know when you hear anything. I'd rather be down there

---Stay there until the sheriff says you're free to go

Piper dropped the phone in her purse and clenched her teeth. *Someone better fix this mess.*

She straightened her scarf and shrugged into the sweater she had dropped on the sofa. Her conference binder lay under the sweater. She sat down and thumbed through the pages of notes and glanced at the invitation. "'Enjoy our relaxing location' . . . " she said. "Ha. I *wish* we had time to relax."

"You mumbling to yourself in here?" Chase breezed through the living room stuffing his arms into his jacket sleeves. "Drone's in the car. Let's go."

Piper followed him to the car, excitement humming through her exhausted body. They had to find a clue to solve the case. She gripped the notebook on her lap and watched the countryside whizz past the window, a prayer filling her heart. *Help us discover the answers, Lord. Please help the doctors and Rosie.*

"The sun will set around seven forty-five. Maybe we should decide between the drone and the island. We can check one tonight and the other tomorrow. Which one?" Chase stretched outside the car.

"The island then," Piper said as she gathered the notebook and her Chanel bag. "How big is this boat?"

"No idea. I told him whatever he has available." He glanced at his watch. "He said he'd meet us here."

"Haydn?" a man called as he hurried down the sidewalk.

Chase waved. The man's gray beard and knit hat gave him the appearance of a sea captain, and Piper hid a smile.

The man nodded in her direction and reached out a hand to Chase. "Boat's over here. Are yous guys planning to be in by sunset? The lights aren't too bright. Pull into this slip here and tie her up. You have use of her 'til tomorrow at five p.m. No funny business. Treat her like she's your own. The insurance policy right here covers any damage, but the deductible is high." He glanced over at Chase and Piper. "You folks look like you're good for it. Supposed to be a tad choppy out there tonight. You sure?"

Chase reached for the clipboard to sign the contract and waivers. "Yes, we're sure. Thank you."

"You pilot a boat before? 'Round here?"

Chase smiled. "We summered in Egg Harbor for years and I learned to sail in Door County. I'm good." He nodded, and the man smiled.

"Have to check, you know. With all the tourists we get, it's hard to know who's prepared and who should hire a captain." He smiled and ripped off a piece of paper. "Yous guys are good to go. Have fun and don't do anything I wouldn't do." He winked and walked away, snickering as he left.

Piper watched him walk down the dock, then turned to Chase. "He reminds me of Rumpelstiltskin. You don't want to mess with his boat. Maybe we should . . ."

Chase stood at the helm of the boat. "Get in. I want to see the island before it gets dark." Piper reached for the hand he held out and stepped into the boat.

"How far?" Piper asked as she settled on the seat behind her brother.

"About a mile. I researched while you got your beauty sleep. The island is part of the park now, but a wealthy family owned it until the Great Depression. The ruins of their summer retreat are still there."

A chill slithered up Piper's spine. "I don't want to explore ruins. I want to find a clue to solve this mystery."

Chase nodded. "But maybe there are clues hiding in the ruins?"

"Worth checking out then," Piper said and jotted a note in the notebook, then tied her scarf over her hair to keep her eyes clear. "Do you think we'll find anything useful, Chase?"

"I hope so, but I don't know. Where else would they go?"

"They could be anywhere by now," Piper said, biting her lip. Worry about Rosie and exhaustion from the past days overwhelmed her. "I want Rosie healthy and all of us back in Cranberry Harbor, living our boring lives."

Chase nodded and grinned. "At least you *admit* our town is boring."

She rolled her eyes and stood as they approached the island. Chase steered the boat to the dock, and Piper scrambled over the side, waiting for him to secure the vessel.

Chase wiped his hands on his jeans and stepped over the side. "Got your phone?"

Piper held her phone up and groaned. "No signal."

"Great," Chase said. "Let's take a quick peek around. We can come back tomorrow. I feel like we should have let someone know where we were going."

"Are you afraid? We can go back."

"No way. I want this over with so we can go see Rosie." He hurried down the trail with Piper close behind.

Piper followed Chase on the path from the dock. The tree canopy dimmed the light, and Piper's skin prickled. She rubbed her arms to warm the goosebumps. "I have a bad feeling, Chase. We should have left the investigation to the sheriff."

"Do you think she planned to investigate? Didn't sound like it from what you told me."

"We gave her our word that we wouldn't do this," Piper said and bent to grab a stick.

"Listen—do you want to go back and sit at the cottage for days while they decide what to do? Or do you want this solved so we can go see Rosie?"

"I want to see my friend, but I'm feeling a bit of trepidation." The melody of Rachmaninoff's "The Isle of the Dead" played in her head, and her goosebumps tingled again. She blew on her hands to warm them and gritted her teeth. *Investigating the island was your idea. Quit being a baby.*

As they walked farther into the dense woods, Piper's heart slammed in her chest. Fear squeezed her mind, and she fought the temptation to run back to the rented boat.

What time I am afraid I will trust in you. What time I am afraid I will trust you.

Chase turned back. "Come on, slowpoke. This is your idea and you're lagging."

Piper caught up to her brother. "Listen—something doesn't feel right. I think—"

"Is that a building?" Chase pointed across a clearing.

"Yes, but anyone inside will see us when we leave the trees." Piper glanced around the clearing. A small limestone building with a damaged roof stood in front of her. Bricks had fallen from the front and lay in a pile on the ground. Broken windows reflected the sun and glittered in the dimming light.

"It's not only my goosebumps, Chase. My hair is standing up too."

"How are you going to be a brilliant detective if you're a scaredy cat?" he teased.

"First, I have no desire to be a detective. I'm a piano teacher in case you forgot. And second, apparently I need Rosie to help me because I can't think straight or solve any of these clues without her."

Chase motioned her to follow him and he continued on the trail. They walked in silence, and Piper stepped carefully to avoid snapping twigs. Chase pointed to the trail in front of him and Piper peered around him to follow his gaze. A hot pink stiletto lay on the path.

"C#," Piper whispered. "That's her shoe."

Chase took a deep breath and whispered. "All right, so we know she was here at least. Let's check out the building." Piper nodded, but her stomach clenched. She didn't want to prowl around a dark building on a deserted island. She wanted to be home in Cranberry Harbor working on her wallpaper project and having no problems bigger than a student refusing to practice scales.

They hurried across the clearing to the ramshackle building, and Chase whispered, "Ready?"

She nodded, and he pushed open the door. As her eyes adjusted to the dim light, she blinked. When her eyes popped open, her stomach sank. "Carolyn!" she yelled.

Slumped in the corner, hands tied behind her back, sat C#. Piper ran around Chase toward her childhood bully. Carolyn's eyes fluttered open and widened. She made a garbled noise around the gag in her mouth. Her matted hair hung to her shoulders, and black streaks of mascara ran down her face. Piper tugged at the gag and finally pulled the fabric loose.

"Carolyn, what happened?"

"You need to get out of here before he comes back." Her voice rasped, and she took a deep breath.

"Who? Before *who* comes back?" Carolyn's eyes fluttered shut, and Piper turned to Chase. "Help me. We need to get her to a hospital. *Who's* coming back, Carolyn?"

Chase reached down and scooped up Carolyn. She slumped in his arms, her head flopped over Chase's elbow. He turned to the door and hurried down the trail.

"Hurry, Chase. Hurry."

Piper glimpsed the rented boat. "We're almost there, Chase." She nudged her brother.

He huffed out a breath. "Going as fast as I can."

"We have to get her on that boat and get out of here before someone comes back."

Chase slid on some pine needles on the path and Piper's heart lurched. He righted himself and they hurried along.

"Almost there, Chase!" she called. A pain stabbed her side, but she hurried behind her brother and Carolyn. "A few more steps. We're going to make it. Hurry."

"We're going to make it—hurry," a voice mocked from off the trail. Chase and Piper stopped and glanced around.

The hair on the back of Piper's neck prickled, and a sob escaped.

"There, there. Don't cry," the voice said. "Set her down and raise your hands."

"I'm continuing to the boat. This woman needs medical care," Chase said, and he took a step forward. A bullet zinged the path in front of his feet.

Piper screamed, and Chase yelled. "Who's there? Show yourself."

Two figures stepped onto the path in front of them, blocking their way to the boat.

"Scott?" Piper frowned.

"Sheriff?" Chase asked.

"Don't move," the sheriff said, pointing the gun at Chase's chest. "I told you not to investigate this island. What are you doing here?"

"We wanted to find clues to solve this murder so we can get to Madison," Piper said. She stood with her arms crossed and scowled. "Why don't you want Carolyn to have medical care? Why haven't you called for help?"

"Listen—you're not the one asking questions. Hands in the air like I said. You"—she pointed the gun at Chase—"I told you to set her down and raise your hands in the air. Do it."

Chase leaned over and gently laid C# on the ground. She moaned and her eyes closed.

"She needs help," he said.

"I'll decide who needs what. Now turn around and march back up the path."

"Scott, what do you have to do with this?" Piper asked.

He grinned, but his smile didn't meet his eyes. "None of your concern."

"He's my brother Carl," Carolyn said.

Carl kicked at Carolyn, and she whimpered.

"Stop it!" Chase yelled and lunged for the man. A bullet zinged past Piper's ear and lodged in a tree in front of her.

Chase whirled around. "What's going on?" he yelled. "Why are you shooting? Put the gun down!"

"Shut up," Sheriff Marks said. "Up the path. Move."

Carl leaned forward and scooped up Carolyn. She moaned. "Shut up."

Piper's heart slammed against her chest. *If the sheriff is involved, we're in deep trouble.* She tripped on a tree root but righted herself before the sheriff yelled at her.

When the group reached the building, the sheriff waved her gun, herding them through the door. Carl dropped Carolyn into the corner where Chase and Piper had found her. She groaned and her eyes flickered open.

The sheriff took water from a shelf and poured it into paper cups. "Here. Drink."

Chase and Piper gulped down the water. "Let me help Carolyn get a drink," Piper said.

The sheriff nodded, and Piper went to help Carolyn. "Come on. Take a sip," she said.

Carolyn sipped at the water and pulled away, leaning her head on the wall.

"You two turn around. Hands behind your backs." The sheriff pulled handcuffs off her belt and cuffed the two Haydns. "Sit in the corners opposite each other," she directed.

Carl tied their feet together and shoved a cloth in their mouths. He pulled Piper's gag and tied it behind her head, pulling her hair as he tugged on the ends of the cloth. She winced and moved her head, but he tugged harder.

"I wish you had listened to me. I don't need this," the sheriff said as she walked through the door. Carl followed behind and slammed the door.

Piper closed her eyes and listened as they locked the door from the outside. She glanced around the room. Small openings lined the ceiling to let in light, but the high stone walls kept them from escaping through a window. *If I sit on Chase's shoulders, I might reach the latch.* Chase worked on his gag and Carolyn leaned against the wall with her eyes closed. What was going on? Scott was her brother Carl? Why would her brother brutalize her? She willed Chase to loosen his gag and hurry to rescue her. Then they would force Carolyn awake and figure out why the sheriff left them as hostages on a deserted island.

Piper sat up and gasped. Her heart thudded in her chest.

"It's me," Chase said. "You fell asleep."

Piper tried to swallow around the fabric in her mouth and willed Chase to hurry. She leaned her head forward as he tugged the knot. Several moments later the fabric fell from Piper's mouth.

"Thank you," she whispered.

"Check your wrists. My handcuffs aren't locked. Try yours."

He pulled, and the handcuffs on her wrist opened.

"Why didn't she lock them?"

"I don't know. She probably didn't think we'd get the gag out of our mouths."

"I need water," Piper said.

"Let me try to untie your feet," Chase said. "Can you believe the sheriff is involved? What do you think is going on?"

"I don't know, Chase. It's so odd. Carl followed me around the piano teachers conference, but he told me his name was Scott. And C# says he's her brother. But if he's her brother, why is he tying her up?" She rubbed her eyes and yawned. "It's so dark out there."

Chase nodded. "Okay, last knot. Let me help you up." He pulled her to her feet on shaky legs. "Do you remember her having a brother?"

Piper nodded. "Yeah, she had a couple at least. I don't remember how many kids in the family."

Chase hurried to the corner and untied Carolyn. He patted her cheeks and called, "Wake up! Come on!"

Piper stretched her numb legs and hands, then poured water for each of them. She trickled water onto Carolyn's head. Her eyes flew open, and she shuddered. "I'm sorry, Carolyn, but we needed you to wake up. What is going on? Why are we locked in here? And why did that man say his name is Scott when you say his name is Carl?"

"He's my brother Carl," she said, and her voice croaked.

"Yes, but why is he treating you like this? What's going on?"

Chase squatted next to them. "That's not right, you know. Brothers don't tie up and hurt their sisters."

Carolyn turned her head away, and a tear trickled down her cheek. "Not every family is like you Haydns," she whispered.

"Hey," Chase said, reaching for her hand. "Tell us. Why is this happening?"

Carolyn took a deep breath. "She's his girlfriend."

"Who? The sheriff?" Piper asked.

Carolyn nodded.

"What are they involved in? Who killed your husband?" Chase asked.

"He's not my husband. He's my brother Clifford."

"What? He said he was your husband. You said he was your husband."

Carolyn snorted. "Part of the con."

Chase glanced at Piper and she touched her finger to her lips to shush him.

"Let me explain," Carolyn said as she told a story of a stolen diamond and lives spent plotting to retrieve the jewel.

Piper leaned against the wall, her eyes wide as C# finished the sordid tale.

"And as you can probably tell, they cut me out of the whole thing and left me here to suffer."

"Will they come back soon?" Piper asked.

Carolyn rolled her eyes. "I can't say. I didn't expect any of this."

"Well, Carolyn, what do you expect when you help criminals?"

Carolyn stared at Piper for a moment and her eyes hardened. "Right—because we all have Piper Haydn's perfect life."

"What is your problem with me?" Piper jumped to her feet and walked toward C#.

Chase patted her arm. "Let it go, sis."

Piper rubbed her eyes and inhaled. "Right. We need to concentrate on getting out of here before they come back."

"How are we getting off the island?" Carolyn asked.

Chase held up the boat key. "We rented a boat. If it's still there, we can get back to the mainland. Who do we call about the sheriff?"

"First things first, Chase. How are we getting out of here?" They had already pushed against the door, which didn't give. The windows high above the floor seemed too far to reach. Hopelessness wrapped around Piper's heart and she sank to the ground in her corner. "Should we attempt to sleep tonight and figure out a plan in the morning?"

"It doesn't matter what you do. You're not getting out."

Piper lifted her chin and stared at C#. "We're getting out of here somehow. Someone will come for us."

Carolyn laughed and coughed. She leaned her head on the wall. "I'm sorry," she whispered.

"What?" Piper asked.

"I said I'm sorry. I'm sorry my brothers are so wretched and I'm sorry I went along with them and I'm sorry that you got wrapped up in the middle." She closed her eyes and leaned on the wall. "I don't hate you, you know."

"Well, that's a surprise, Carolyn."

"I don't. I'm jealous. I've always been jealous of you. Even now your brother is here with you, helping you and trying to take care of you. My family consists of cheats and crooks. We don't even trust each other." A tear trickled down her cheek. "I'd give anything to have someone in my family care about me."

Piper's heart squeezed, and she glanced at Chase. He made a pout face and Piper smiled at him. She took a deep breath and swallowed. The frustration from C#'s childhood antics and her fear of their situation melted away.

"I'm sorry, Carolyn, that your family has left you feeling unloved. My family's love and support are something I've always thanked the Lord for, and I can't imagine living without them. I can't change anything for you, but I want you to know that your hurt saddens me. I also want you to know that I forgive you for all the things you did when we were young."

C# opened her mouth and closed it. Tears trickled down her cheeks, and she nodded. "Thank you," she whispered.

Chase clapped his hands together. "Okay, ladies, now that the boo-hooing is done, time to get serious about getting out of here. At least we can plan what we're going to do to them when they come back."

Piper rolled her eyes, and C# giggled.

"You in, C#? You're not going to turn on us and help them?" Chase asked.

"You're kidding right?"

Chase narrowed his eyes. "I don't know. I don't really know you."

Piper winked at Carolyn. "We should trust her, Chase. The C# I knew wouldn't apologize if she didn't mean it and I don't think the grown-up C# is any different. Let's get busy. We have crooks to outmaneuver."

CHAPTER 10

Tuesday

Piper leaned her head on her brother's side. She slept, but her mind raced. Her neck ached from the odd position, and the stone floor chilled her bones. She shifted to rest her head on Chase's leg. Using her brother as a pillow beat lying flat on the cement floor.

Chase snored a soft whiffling sound and shifted closer to the wall. C# sprawled on the floor and snored like a freight train. Piper rubbed her eyes and inhaled. They planned to break free tomorrow morning or rush C#'s brother when he came back. Either way, she needed rest.

Lord, what are we doing? He brought a gun last time. I don't want anyone else getting hurt. Please rescue us before something terrible happens.

She drifted into a fitful sleep dreaming of guns, imposter piano teachers, terror, and boats. She and Chase moved C# into the boat and took off, but Scott—or Carl—followed close behind, shooting at their boat. Piper and Carolyn huddled in the cabin below deck and Chase hollered at their enemies using pirate talk.

"Hey, Pip," Chase whispered. "You're screaming."

Piper pushed off her brother's legs and stretched. "Sorry. Bad dream. What time is it?"

"I don't know. It's pretty dark still. Two? Three? Can you sleep?"

"If I can lean on you again."

He wrapped his arm around her and pulled her close. "I'm sorry I got you into this. I'm such a mess-up."

Piper patted Chase's leg. "You're not a mess-up, Chase. I wanted to come along as badly as you did. It's nobody's fault but the person doing this to us. Let's get some sleep so we can bust out of here tomorrow."

"I don't know how we will get off the island without being seen," he whispered.

"Shh. We can't worry about tomorrow yet. Go to sleep."

Birds chirping in the tree outside the window woke Piper. She sat up and groaned. Her bones ached and the muscles in her neck spasmed. She reached her hands above her head to stretch and rolled her neck from side to side. She groaned as she pulled herself off the floor.

Chase rubbed his eyes and grinned. "All the creaking sounds like you're ready for the rocking chair."

"Oh, you're the funny one." Piper reached out a hand to help him stand. "All right, commander. What's the plan?"

"You're going to boost me up and I'm going to pull myself through that window. I'll go down and see if the boat is still there. If not, I'll walk around the island and search the island for other people who might help us. If I get to the mainland, I'll call Chief Maxwell and tell him about the corrupt sheriff. He'll know what to do. Can you and Carolyn wait here, no matter how long I take?"

Carolyn snorted from the corner. "I can barely move. You don't need to worry about me."

Piper hurried over to C# with a glass of water. "Are you okay?"

C# laughed. "No, I'm not, but I'll survive. I hope my idiot brother comes back before I get worse."

"How did you plan to pull this heist off?" Piper asked.

"First of all, I didn't expect my brother to double-cross me. I didn't expect the sheriff to get involved. I didn't expect Rosie to burst out of the camper. We were supposed to dig up the jewel and be on our way to happily ever after."

"Where would you sell it? Isn't the jewel recognizable?"

C# rolled her eyes. "Certain people don't buy and sell by the rules. Carl found a buyer, but who knows if anything he said is true? He and the sheriff have something personal going on."

"Who shot Rosie?" Chase asked.

"The sheriff. Rosie fought when Carl tried to carry her onto the boat. She whipped around like a bucking bronco. She bit his shoulder and kicked the sheriff in the face. Carl told her to shut up, but she didn't." C# chuckled. "That girl always had spunk. The sheriff shot her in the shoulder and told Carl to dump her under the overhang. The sheriff was angry about the time he took to hide her—it messed with her schedule somehow. She was livid after that."

"Well, I'm angry she shot my friend," Piper said as her stomach clenched and she swallowed the bile rising in her throat.

"Shooting Rosie wasn't part of the plan. You guys showing up here also isn't part of the plan. I don't know what they'll do to get back on track, but I don't think they'll play nice."

"Aren't you angry your brother cut you out of the deal?"

Carolyn stared at Piper for several moments. "Yeah, I'm angry. Angry that I didn't think of shooting him first." She laughed a high-pitched cackling laugh. "Our family is all Norman Rockwell, you know. It's no surprise that he'd do something stupid."

"We have to work together against them."

Carolyn nodded.

"Help me up," Chase said. He waited under the windows. She cupped her hands, and he stepped on her.

"Oof, Chase. Hurry. I can't hold you very long. What have you been eating?"

"Junk food. All right, I'm grabbing the ledge—don't let go yet." He pushed out the window and pulled himself up to the ledge.

Piper wiggled her hands and rubbed her fingers, wincing at the pain. She glanced up in time to see her brother wave and disappear through the window. She breathed a quick prayer and turned to Carolyn. "The Duchess really vacationed in Door County?" Piper asked.

"Yes, her first husband and his family owned a summer home here. She spent the summer in Ephraim and befriended a local girl. The wedding invitation Wallis sent to Liz is in the museum."

"That's what Rosie wanted to show me, but I didn't have time to check it out. How did the museum get a diamond from a duchess?"

Carolyn smiled. "A gift Wallis Simpson sent her friend years later. After Liz's death, her family donated her belongings to the museum where my dad worked." A grin spread across her face and she leaned on the wall. "He spent years working on outsmarting their security system and finally stole the stone."

"He buried it in the park and . . . ?"

"Then he and mom disappeared and changed their names. He always planned to come back and dig them up, but he died of a heart attack when I was young. My brothers have plotted how to recover the diamond for decades," she said. "Not sure it's worth all this."

"I'm sure the diamond is worth a fortune, isn't it?"

C# nodded. "Yes. The diamond belonged to the Duchess of Windsor, even if she wasn't royalty yet. I imagine people would pay big bucks to own something she touched."

"Piper!" Chase called from outside and she hurried under the open window to listen.

"What?"

"I don't see any way to get back in or to let you out!"

"Is the boat still there?"

"I didn't get that far!"

"Okay!" she hollered. "Go check on the boat and come back and tell us!"

"On it!" he called back.

Piper stood with her hands on her hips, scrutinizing the room. "Chase is correct. The only way out is through the door or through the window way up there. I won't worry until he comes back and tells me the rental boat is gone."

Carolyn nodded and closed her eyes.

Piper slid to the floor across from her old nemesis. "Carolyn, did you ever wish you would grow up and marry a prince?"

"The girly princess stuff and all that?" Carolyn whispered. "Yeah."

"Nope. I knew and my family made sure I knew that I was nothing special. I always wished I grew up in a family like yours."

A lump rose in Piper's throat, and tears stung her eyes. "Oh, Carolyn." She coughed to cover the tremble in her voice.

"Your family treated you like a princess every day, and I was always so jealous of you. You and Rosie flaunted your precious friendship. I hated you."

Piper nodded and dabbed tears from her eyes. "I always wondered why you were so unkind to me, but I understand now. I'm sorry your family didn't cherish you."

Carolyn waved her hand. "Old news. It's not like anything's ever going to change. As you can see, my brother tied me up here and killed my other brother. Best I can hope for is a shorter sentence if I cooperate."

Tears rolled down Piper's cheeks. She remembered all the times she returned Carolyn's unkindness instead of showing her the love of Jesus. Even these past days at the conference, she had spoken to her rudely. "I'm sorry I didn't see past everything and treat you right."

"We were kids. Piper. I'm sure I would have punched you if you were kind to me." She laughed and rolled her eyes.

"Well, C#, I don't think you're as bad as you've led us to believe all these years."

"Thanks, princess," Carolyn smiled. "That means a lot coming from you."

"I'm sure Chase will rescue us."

"Keep believing and all that, huh?"

Piper nodded, but her stomach twisted in knots. If Chase didn't save them, they would have to wait for C#'s brother and the sheriff to return, and that terrified Piper. "Who would have imagined the sheriff was involved?"

C# snorted. "Oh, princess—you got a lot to learn."

Piper stood and paced, waiting for her brother to return. *Oh, Lord—we need You.*

A scuffle at the door stopped Piper's pacing. Carolyn's eyes widened, and she stared at Piper. "Chase," she mouthed.

Piper stood facing the door. She glanced around, searching for something to grab in case she needed to hit someone upside the head. A water jug stood on the ledge near her, but a plastic jug was worthless as a weapon.

The door popped open, and Chase stood in the frame.

"Chase!" both women yelled.

He stumbled over the threshold as C#'s brother Carl pushed him through the door. The sheriff followed with her gun pointed at the group.

Piper's optimism crashed, and she bit her lip to hold back tears. She braced herself when Carl shoved Chase to her corner.

"All right," the sheriff said. "I told you to stay out of my investigation and you didn't listen. I'm arresting you two and taking you back to Sturgeon Bay. You"—she waved the gun at Carl—"take your sister to their boat and get her to a hospital in Michigan. Marinette is across from here." She pointed the gun at Piper and Chase as Carl handcuffed their hands.

Piper's stomach lurched, and she shuddered. The gun pointed at her heart didn't ease her fear that she and Chase would survive this ordeal. "Listen," she said. "Let us go. We won't say a word. We'll take the boat back to the rental shop and go on our way. Let us take Carolyn. You and Carl can go dig up the diamond and escape."

The sheriff's eyes narrowed, and she raised the gun to Piper's head. "Shut up!" she yelled. "Move!" She waved the gun, and Carl shoved them toward the door.

Piper glanced back at her childhood enemy and said, "I'm sorry."

Carolyn nodded and smiled a thin smile as Carl scooped her from the floor.

"Shut up!" The sheriff poked the gun in her back and Piper walked through the door into the sunlight with Chase close behind.

Piper stumbled down the pine needle-covered trail, scrambling to stay a step ahead of the sheriff and her gun.

"Move it—we don't have time to waste," Sheriff Marks ordered.

Piper forced her shaky legs to move faster, but her balance was off with her hands behind her back. "I'm trying," she said. Her breath huffed out in painful blasts. *I need to take up running when this is over. I should not be huffing and puffing like this.*

Piper glimpsed the Door County Sherriff's boat straight ahead. Perhaps getting arrested and taken back to civilization wasn't all bad. The department must have honest officers. Someone would blow the whistle on the corrupt sheriff. She would hang on to hope long enough to get back to the jail. She would tell anyone who would listen, or she would call Lenny. Lenny would fix this. She breathed a sigh of relief. Yes, that's what she would do and everything would work out fine.

"Stop," the sheriff called.

Piper stood still, and the sheriff pushed past her on the path.

"I'll walk out on the dock first. You two follow. If you do anything other than get in the boat, I will shoot you. Understand?" She stared at Chase and Piper, and they nodded. "Step down onto the dock and we will get in the boat one at a time."

Piper stepped toward the dock and slipped on the wet wood. With her hands in handcuffs and no way to help herself, she landed face down, hanging over the water and sliding toward the edge. Her toes dug into the wood, but the momentum threatened to pull her into the water. Her heart pounded, and she gulped for air. Spots floated in front of her eyes. *Please, God—send help.*

"Raise your hands in the air," a voice called from the forest. Footsteps pounded down the path and the sheriff fell across Piper. The woods echoed with barked orders and yelling. The wood from the dock pressed a sliver into Piper's cheek and her lungs screamed for air.

Someone lifted the sheriff off her back, and an arm pulled her to her feet. A helicopter roared overhead, and an officer leaned out the open door. "This is the Wisconsin Department of Criminal Investigation. Cooperate with the officers on the ground."

Piper's eyes widened, and she glanced around the dock and the path to the building where the sheriff had held her hostage. The area swarmed with officers and one of them handcuffed Sheriff Marks. "You have the right to remain silent . . ."

Piper's head throbbed as she eavesdropped on Chase's conversation with an officer near him. Another officer ran down the trail carrying C#, and Piper's eyes stung with tears. "You're going to be okay!" she called. C# gave her a halfhearted thumbs-up. She turned back to the scene on the dock as a boat pulled up and officers poured over the side. Will jumped out of the boat and ran for Piper. A sob rose in her throat, and he wrapped his arms around her shoulders, helping her sit on the dock as he unlocked her handcuffs.

Piper rested her hand on her chest and squeezed her eyes shut. The nausea in her stomach combined with the relief at seeing a familiar face left her dizzy and speechless. The officers continued shouting orders and moving around the island.

"How did you know?"

"Rosie told us. We texted you."

"We didn't have reception. Rosie? Please tell me she's okay." Piper opened her eyes and searched Will's face. "Don't lie to me."

"She's making good progress, and the doctor says she will recover completely. They transferred her to Cranberry Harbor today."

Tears poured down Piper's face, and she sobbed. All the worry and fear from the past days pounded in her heart while she cried.

Will pulled her close to his side and patted her back. "I'm sorry we didn't know the sheriff was corrupt before we left Door County. If I'd known, I never would have left you here alone."

Piper nodded and dabbed at her nose with her sleeve. She grimaced at the mess and Will laughed. "Here," he said, holding out his leg. "Wipe it on my jeans. I don't mind."

Piper wiped her sleeve on his jeans and grinned. "Sorry."

He smiled. "I've dealt with worse."

An officer stepped onto the dock. "Let's get these two back to Sturgeon Bay and interview them so they can rest."

Will helped Piper to her feet and into the boat. "Call me when you're done and I'll get you two back to the cottage."

"No," Piper said. "We're going home to see Rosie. I can't wait a minute longer than necessary."

Will smiled. "Absolutely." He hurried to the boat with the other officers while the officer with Piper guided her to the Door County Sheriff's boat. She climbed over the side with help from Chase and sank onto the bench. Chase dropped into the seat next to her and leaned his head into his hands.

"I've never been so scared in my life," he whispered.

"Me too."

He rubbed his face and sat up. "It's almost over. We survived."

Piper smiled a thin smile. "That remains to be seen, dear brother. I'm quite a wreck right now."

He nodded. "Me too. But we're safe."

She patted his leg and leaned on the seat behind her, falling asleep before the boat pulled away from the dock.

Lenny waited at the Door County Sheriff's Department.

Piper climbed out of the police cruiser and yawned. "Oh, Lenny—my soul is tired." She adjusted her scarf and fluffed her hair. "How do I look? Like I spent the night as a hostage?"

Lenny smiled and held the door open for her. "The officers have assured me this part will be brief. Then we'll get you home to rest."

"Is Rosie in Cranberry Harbor?"

Lenny glanced at his watch. "She's supposed to arrive in the next few minutes, but by the time you get home, visiting hours might have ended."

"If visiting hours are over, I'm still seeing her." A lump rose in her throat and she turned away.

"Hey," Lenny said. "Keep your chin up, kid."

Piper gave him a thumbs-up and entered the building.

Chase elbowed her. "At least we're not suspects this time."

Piper rolled her eyes. "Rather baffling that they ever suspected us. As if I'm capable of hurting Rosie." She swallowed over the lump in her throat.

"Hey, like Lenny said, 'Keep your chin up, kid.'"

The officer ushered the three of them into a room and shut the door. "Let's get this over with and get you on your way home," the officer said.

Piper raised her hands in the air and said, "Hallelujah!"

CHAPTER 11

Tuesday Evening

When they approached Cranberry Harbor, Chase tapped Piper's knee. She opened one eye and groaned. "What?"

"Hey, Pip. You slept the entire way home. Getting your beauty sleep?"

"I slept for three hours?" Piper adjusted herself in the seat and yawned. "I'm so tired."

"Should I drop you off at your house? We can visit Rosie tomorrow."

"No. Absolutely not. We're stopping at the hospital right now."

"Do you want to freshen up?"

"No, I know I am dirty and I smell, but I have to see her." Her voice wobbled, and she turned her head to the window.

"Hey. It's okay. I get it," Chase whispered. "I'll wait in the waiting room until you ask her if I have permission to visit."

Piper ran her fingers through her hair and dug through her bag for gum. "Need a piece?"

Chase held his hand out and she dropped a stick of gum in his hand and popped another one into her mouth.

"That's as good as it's gonna get. Now take me to Roosevelt."

"Yes, ma'am," Chase said and stepped on the accelerator.

Piper smiled and rubbed the grit from her tired eyes. "Don't get a ticket."

"Not me." Chase said with a grin.

Lights flashed behind them, and Piper groaned. "Are you kidding me?"

Chase's tires crunched on the gravel as he pulled his Tesla to the side of the road and rolled the window down.

The officer leaned down to the window and smiled. "Hey, are you on your way to the hospital to see Rosie?"

"Yes, why? Is something wrong?" Piper leaned across Chase to address the officer.

"No, but Chief Maxwell asked us to keep our eyes peeled for you and escort you to the hospital. Follow me. I'll take you straight to the front door."

Piper smiled. "Thank you, sir."

He nodded and hurried to his car.

"Well, there's a perk of small-town living," Piper said. "Follow that man."

Chase pulled onto the road behind the officer and followed the flashing lights.

Chase stopped his car at the front door of the hospital, and Piper jumped out. She scrambled through the front doors and ran to the reception desk.

"Roosevelt Hale's room number, please."

A white-haired woman in a pink smock puttered behind the desk, tapping keys on a keyboard.

Piper bit her lip to stop herself from asking the woman to hurry.

The woman lifted her glasses to the top of her head and squinted. "Oh, my," she said, laughing. "I can't see a thing. Mabel, come read this for me."

Piper bit her lip and considered jumping over the desk to read the room number for herself.

Another pink-smocked woman stepped to the desk and leaned over. She squinted and lifted her glasses. "Hill?"

"No, Hale." Piper plastered a sweet smile on her lips. *Help me keep my mouth shut, Lord.*

"Hull . . . here we go. Room 343." She stood straight and smiled at Piper. "You have a delightful visit now, sweetheart."

Piper inhaled and smiled. "I believe you said 'Hull.' Can you please double-check for Hale?"

She chuckled. "My hearing's not so great, honey. I'm sorry. So, Hail, you say. Like in a storm?"

Piper plastered another smile on her face, resisting the urge to roar at the lady. "Can you try Hale? Like Nathan Hale, the founding father?"

"Oh! *Hale.* Why didn't you say so in the first place?" She leaned over the other woman and traced across the computer monitor with her finger. "Room 416."

"Thank you," Piper said as she ran to the elevator and punched the button.

"It doesn't come down any faster no matter how many times you push the button, dear," the woman named Mabel called down the hall.

Piper flicked a thumbs-up to the woman and gritted her teeth. She glanced around the hallway for the stairwell, but the elevator dinged and the doors opened.

A family stepped into the elevator, and a little boy pushed the two and three buttons.

"Jonathan, we are going to *four*." His mother nudged him away from the panel.

Piper bit her tongue and inhaled a deep breath.

"Are you okay, lady?" the little boy asked as he stood near her knee, watching her.

Piper pasted on a cheesy smile and nodded at the boy. He stared at her as the doors opened and closed on the second and third floors. When the elevator opened on the fourth floor, Piper bolted to the open door, but the stroller wheel caught blocking her exit. The boy pushed the remaining buttons on the keypad and stared at Piper while his parents worked the wheel loose.

A silent wail rose in her throat, but she bit her tongue. As a Haydn in Cranberry Harbor, she wasn't allowed to unleash her frustration on the little ladies at the reception desk or on slow-moving families. Her dad would throw a fit if a Haydn displayed rude behavior. When the stroller wheel popped free, the dad moved enough for Piper to squeeze through the opening. She bolted from the elevator, checked the room number signs, and followed the arrows to Rosie's room.

At the closed door she straightened her scarf and took a deep breath. She knocked and gently nudged the door open.

Rosie lay across from the door, her red curls spread across the pillow. Piper's heart lurched as she tiptoed into the room. She sat in the empty chair beside the bed and pulled Rosie's hand into hers.

Rosie's eyes opened and she smiled. "It's you."

"Of course it's me," Piper said. A tear trickled down her cheek and the lump in her throat grew.

"None of that," Rosie whispered. "They expect a complete recovery. I'm groggy from the extra pain meds for the ambulance ride." She turned her head and a soft snore filled the room.

Piper leaned back in her chair, holding her friend's hand, and closed her eyes.

Please, God—let that be true. Help her heal as quickly as possible.

A hand nudged Piper's shoulder, and she startled. "Sorry to scare you, miss, but visiting hours are over. You need to head home. We'll see you in the morning."

"Is she going to be okay?" Piper whispered.

"She is. She's sleeping now because her body needs to rest, but she's doing good. Don't worry. I'm watching over her tonight and the good Lord is too. You need to sleep."

Piper tiptoed out of the room and found Chase in the waiting room. He reached for her as she fell into his arms and sobbed.

"Hey—bad news?"

"No. I'm happy. She's going to be fine." Piper dabbed her eyes and smiled. "She's going to be fine."

Chase smiled, and tears glistened in his eyes. "Come on—let's get you home. I'm sure you'll drive over here the minute visiting hours start tomorrow. Will you do your brother a favor?"

"Hmm?"

"Give me a chance to see her too."

Piper nodded. "We'll see. Bring me coffee and anything is possible." Her phone buzzed, and she checked her messages.

--*I'm waiting at your house to tuck you in.*

Piper smiled and tucked the phone back into her Chanel bag.

"Good news?" Chase asked.

"Mom's waiting to tuck me in."

"Nice. Who's tucking *me* in?"

Piper laughed. "Not sure, buddy. If you want to stay at my house, I'm sure she'll tuck you in too."

Chase rolled his eyes. "I'm not sleeping in that wreck until you get it fixed."

"Hey!"

"*Someone* has to say it, Pip."

Piper playfully punched his arm. "I'm glad you were with me. Not glad you went through this too, but I'm glad I wasn't alone."

Chase nodded. "Same."

"Are we going to have PTSD over this?"

"Probably."

"I'll see my counselor. You need a recommendation?"

"Nah. I'm fine."

"Surprising what a good chat with a licensed professional can do for you."

Chase patted her leg. "Thanks. Don't worry about me, okay?"

Piper reached out and squeezed her brother's hand. "I do worry about you, but I'll try to let you take care of yourself."

"Thanks. You're home." He leaned over and kissed her cheek. "Get some rest. Do you want a ride in the morning?"

"Are you stopping at Ruby's and bringing me her tallest latte?"

"Sure."

"Perfect. See you in the morning."

Chase's headlights lit her path to the door, and a lamp in her living room spilled warm light onto the porch. Weariness flooded her as she pushed open the front door, but her mother stood inside and wrapped her arms around Piper in a comforting hug.

Tears stung her eyes as she melted into her mother's arms. "I'm so glad I'm home."

Sarah Haydn kissed her forehead. "Oh, sweetheart. Me too. I stayed awake until Chief Maxwell called and said you were safe. Let's get you in the shower and I'll tuck you in. I'm staying here with you tonight." Her mother led her up the staircase and Piper dragged behind.

"I'm so tired, Mom. I should go straight to bed."

"If you took a peek at yourself in the mirror, you'd agree with me, darling. Rinse off at least and let the hot water work its magic. I'll wait in your room."

Piper obeyed and climbed into the tub to rinse before collapsing on her bed. Sarah Haydn tucked a soft comforter around Piper and pulled the blanket to her chin. She pushed the hair back from Piper's face and leaned down to kiss her cheek.

"Piper Haydn," her mother whispered in her ear. "Never scare me like that again."

Piper smiled and turned on her side while her mother rubbed her back until she drifted off to dreamland.

CHAPTER 12

Wednesday

Piper woke early and hurried to dress. She slipped into a white pencil skirt and pink sweater set and tied a pale blue scarf around her neck. She puffed the fabric around the knot into a flower shape and tugged a brush through her hair. Chase's horn sounded as she finished. She slipped her feet into a pair of flats and hurried down the stairs.

Chase leaned on the horn for the second time right as Piper opened her front door. She scowled at her brother but hurried to the car before he blared the horn again.

"Chase, you know Mother will have your head for honking at a lady."

Chase snorted. "You're my sister, Pip. You're not a lady. Here's your coffee." He handed her an extra-large latte from Ruby's.

Piper sipped the hot liquid. "Mmm. I missed these." She pointed to the road. "Let's go, brother. I need to see Roosevelt."

"You'll ask if I can see her too?"

"Of course," Piper said and gulped her coffee.

Chase dropped her off at the hospital doors. "Text me if she says yes. I'll wait here a while just in case."

Piper hopped out of the Tesla with her coffee and her purse. She hurried through the doors, bypassing the desk. She knew where to find Rosie and this time she took the stairs. No little kid pushing all the numbers to slow her down.

Despite all her huffing and puffing, she climbed the stairs in record time and opened the door to the fourth floor. Doctors and nurses ran past, and a loud beeping sounded in the hall. Piper's heart pounded, and she glanced toward Rosie's end of the hall. No commotion. She hurried down to Rosie's room and knocked.

"Come in."

When Piper pushed open the door, Rosie sat upright in bed, wearing a turban covered in pink silk flowers. Bits of her red curls stuck out from the hat, and wooden hoops dangled from her ears. Instead of a hospital gown, she wore a muumuu that matched her turban.

A grin spread across Piper's face. "Well, you must feel better."

Rosie smiled and reached for Piper. "Mom brought these for me this morning and you're right. I feel much better."

Piper leaned over and kissed Rosie's cheek. "Roosevelt Hale, what in the world happened?"

Rosie grunted and leaned her head back on the pillow. "What do you know?"

"Not much. We came straight here last night, but you were so drowsy that you drifted off to sleep, and I needed to rest, so I went home hoping you'd be awake this morning."

Rosie's eyes closed and Piper wondered if she would fall back to sleep, but Rosie sat up and said, "I was asleep on the bunk in the glamper roof when I heard noises. I glanced outside and found three people standing near our fire ring. I considered yelling to scare them off but watched to see what they were doing. My phone didn't have service, or I would have called you." She blew out a breath. "They dug forever, and I recognized the ranger and that Scott dude who followed me at the museum."

"He's the Scott that followed you?" Piper asked. "He's the Scott that followed *me*."

"Creep," Rosie said. "Anyway, I heard them call the girl Carolyn, so I assumed she was C# even though I haven't seen her in years—thank God."

"Sorry to interrupt. I forgot to ask if Chase can come up now."

Rosie nodded, and Piper sent a text to her brother, inviting him to come to Rosie's room.

Rosie leaned back on her pillow. "I don't think they found anything. Do you know what they were searching for?"

"The Duchess' diamond."

Rosie's eyes widened. "I told you about that."

"Yes. If I have the story straight, their dad stole the jewel from the museum decades ago and hid the diamond in the park. They've searched for years and narrowed it down to our campsite."

"My goodness!" Rosie said. "Like I said, I didn't see them find anything. They argued. The ranger stepped to his golf cart and Scott yelled. The next thing I knew, the ranger turned around and they wrestled. I don't know why no one else came, because they were loud. Then Scott pulled out a gun and shot the ranger. I jumped down and slammed the glamper door open." She giggled. "You should have seen their faces. They didn't know I was there."

"Let me interrupt here. The ranger isn't a ranger. He's their brother."

"What?" Rosie shrieked.

The door opened, and a nurse ran in. "Miss, you need to keep the volume down in here. You're still recuperating. If you get too excited, I'll ask your friend to leave."

"Yes, ma'am," Rosie said to the nurse and turned to Piper. "You're kidding me. How did he have a uniform and that ridiculous ticket pad?"

"What happened when you slammed the glamper door open?"

"Their mouths dropped and then Scott roared and ran at me. I tried to use my fancy martial arts moves, but he jerked my foot and I fell. He dragged me out of the glamper and that jerk tore my dress."

"I'm glad because I found the fabric stuck to the hinge on the cupboard. Good clue."

"I didn't leave it on purpose, but I did at the Eagle Tower since he already ruined it. My favorite dress!"

"We can find you a new dress. At least you're alive."

Rosie narrowed her eyes. "I'm glad I'm alive too, but the odds of me finding that dress in a similar fabric are pretty slim, friend."

Piper patted Rosie's hand and smiled. "You must feel better. You're getting spunky. What happened next?"

A knock at the door interrupted the story. Chase pushed the door open and peeked around. "Everybody decent in here?"

"Come here, you big lug," Rosie held out an arm. "Be careful. Don't hurt me."

Chase leaned down and hugged her.

"Thank you for finding me," she said and squeezed Chase's hand. "Sit." She pointed to the chair on the other side of the bed and waited for Chase to get comfortable.

"Where was I? Oh, I don't know how, but the next thing I knew they chained me to the railing on the Eagle Tower."

"With C#?" Piper asked.

"No, I spent that first night alone." She rolled her eyes. "That was an experience. When I woke up in the morning, C# sat tied up to the rail across from me."

"We knew she was there because Piper recognized her pink shoe," Chase said.

"He kept us there all day. I hurt for C#. Her brothers turned on her and they didn't even find the jewel, did they?"

"I don't think so," Piper said. "When did he shoot you?"

Rosie adjusted the flowered turban and sipped her water. She narrowed her eyes. "Did you know the sheriff planned the whole thing? Even getting rid of Scott's siblings." She shivered. "Scott and the sheriff took us down from the tower. At first I hoped the sheriff had come to rescue me. That was a bummer."

Piper patted Rosie's hand. "They planned to take us somewhere on a boat, but I wasn't about to cooperate. Scott carried me and I kicked and bit and pinched. I shrieked and pulled his hair. The sheriff was busy with Carolyn, but she kept yelling at me to shut up."

"His name isn't Scott, by the way. It's Carl. Carl, Clifford, and Carolyn."

Rosie's laughter burst out in a guffaw. "Those are awful boy names. Now we know why he went by 'Scott.'" She wiped her eyes and held her side. "I can't laugh, you guys. It hurts too much."

Piper reached for her friend's hand. "What do you need?"

"I'm fine. Let me finish this story so you can leave and let me sleep." She grinned. "So I kept kicking and biting and pinching and he kept yelling. 'Stop it!' I clamped my jaw on his back and bit with all my might. He roared and dropped me in the sand. I tried to jump up and run away, but the sheriff shot me in my shoulder." She pointed to her shoulder and grimaced. "I wasn't strong enough to get up, of course. Before I passed out, I heard her telling him to hide me and that's the last I remembered until I woke up after surgery."

Piper swallowed the lump in her throat. "I'm so glad Chase found you. I thought you had died."

"Well," Rosie said, fluffing her stray curls. "We won't dwell on that. Chase found me and they got me to the hospital in time to fix me up as good as new. I'll heal and life goes on."

"It does, but you don't have to jump back into everything immediately. I'll give you as much leave as you need."

"Leave? From the academy? No way. Don't you worry about me, girlfriend." She sniffed the air. "Do I smell coffee? You went to Ruby's, didn't you?" She glared at Piper, then turned to Chase. "Who went?"

Chase raised his hand and smiled a cheesy smile. "If they'll let you have one, I'll go back."

"Vamoose," she said, waving her uninjured hand toward the door. "Extra-large with extra cream."

Chase hurried from the room. "I'll see what I can do."

When the door clicked shut, Rosie turned to Piper. "Chief Maxwell sat at the hospital the whole time I was in surgery."

"I'm angry I had to stay behind."

"He told me what happened to you. Maybe you need to take a leave of absence as well."

Piper nodded. "I probably do, but this isn't good timing. It's almost time to open for the school year and I can't afford to close."

"Chief Maxwell is a good guy, Piper."

"I never said he wasn't." Piper dug in her bag, avoiding Rosie's eyes.

Rosie cleared her throat. "Piper?"

"What?"

"He's a good guy, *and* he's hunky."

"Rosie, I asked you to stop."

Rosie grinned. "What? It's true. Chief Maxwell is not an ugly man. He cares about you. When he came to see me yesterday, he seemed extra worried about you. Kind of cute how he avoids saying he likes you, but he can't hide his feelings. His face shows everything he's thinking when he mentions you."

"Rosie," Piper whispered. "Please stop. You know it's too soon."

"What's too soon? Spending time with a decent man? You deserve happiness, and a man who's easy on the eyes sounds wonderful to me."

Piper rolled her eyes. "Speaking of feelings—you know Chase is in love with you."

Rosie turned to the window, but not before Piper noticed the pink rising in her cheeks. She turned back to Piper and said, "I know, and I have feelings for Chase. I've loved him since the day I popped him in the nose for making fun of you." She smiled. "But Chase needs to figure out a lot of things about his life. I will not fix him or save him from his choices. He has to change and grow because he wants to, not to catch me. I won't speak about my feelings to him until he's pulled himself together. So that's that." She smiled at Piper, but a tear glistened in her eye. She wiped it away and adjusted her turban with one hand. "I'm glad you're my friend, Piper Haydn."

"Me too, Roosevelt Hale."

Rosie squeezed her hand and laid her head on the pillow. "If you don't mind, I'm going to snooze until Chase gets back with my coffee."

Piper held Rosie's hand and watched her sleep. *Thank you for sparing her, Lord. I need her in my life to remind me to seek joy and beauty. Help her heal and help her keep her joy.*

A knock at the door interrupted her prayer. "Come in, Chase."

"I'm not Chase, but I hope you'll let me come in." Chief Maxwell stood in the doorway with a balloon. "I brought this for Rosie. This room seems a little bland for Miss Hale's taste." He smiled a lopsided grin and winked at Piper.

Her cheeks flooded with heat, and she cleared her throat. "You've figured her out."

"Yes, Miss Hale is the colorful artistic one of you two." He tied the balloon to the side table and turned to Piper. "Am I right?"

"Yes. I guess I'm the boring one."

"I didn't say that," Chief Maxwell said. His eyes searched hers until she glanced away.

Her stomach fluttered, and she bit her lip. *What in the world?*

His soft chuckle filled her ears, and she glanced back at the officer. He smiled at her and winked again.

"I'm on duty. I stopped to brighten up her room. Tell her I visited, please."

"Of course," Piper said. He turned to leave but stopped at the door. "Glad you're safe, Miss Haydn. I wasn't able to sleep until we found you. I . . ." He stopped to clear his throat and left before he finished the sentence.

Piper stared at the closed door long after he stepped into the hall, wanting to know what he meant to say and curious about the butterflies fluttering in her stomach every time Chief Will Maxwell smiled.

CHAPTER 13

Coda: One month later

Piper sat in her turret, sheet music scattered across the floor. She matched the Rachmaninoff pieces to her senior students and penciled practice notes on the cover of each piece. The school year was in full swing, and regardless of how much Piper longed for rest, work at the academy piled up.

The wallpaper project still waited for Rosie to gain use of her arm. When Rosie found out Piper had searched for a contractor to finish the wallpaper, she threw a fit. "Piper, that's *my* project. Please wait until I can finish." Piper relented. Living with the mess beat dealing with a cranky Rosie.

A knock at the front door interrupted her sorting and note-writing. Jack Haydn waited on the porch, and Piper smiled a cheesy smile. "I'm in the middle of a project, Dad, but things are not as bad as they appear."

Jack Haydn stepped into the turret and whistled. "Interesting aesthetic, Piper Grace. This is hideous. How can you live in this dump?"

"Dad, my precious house isn't a dump. Rosie tore off all this wallpaper before our ill-fated glamping trip and made me promise to let her finish when she's healed. After everything she's been through, saying no isn't an option

Jack laughed. "You two are a pair. I won't say any more unless this project drags on."

Piper stood on her tiptoes and kissed his cheek. "We will finish, Daddy. Now, why did you stop?"

"I stopped to tell you we got the go-ahead for the cherry barbecue chips. Braden found a factory in Idaho that will private-label and use our recipe."

"Wonderful news, Dad. They are yummy."

He glanced around the room and rolled his eyes. "Tell me when you get this done," he said and wiggled his foot to loosen the wallpaper stuck to his leather loafer. "I'll come back when it's safe."

Piper rolled her eyes. "Someday all the work will get done and you'll beg me to live here."

Jack Haydn chuckled and wrapped his arms around Piper. He kissed the top of her head and said, "Keep dreaming, baby girl."

Piper waved as he backed out of her driveway, then returned to her work matching recital music with the abilities of her ten senior students. She considered their strengths and scribbled notes. When she hit "play" on her phone, the notes of Rachmaninoff's "Opus 21 No. 7, How Fair Is the Spot" filled the room. She leaned her head on the couch cushion and listened to the peaceful music until the urge to play the piece herself overtook her urge to rest.

She pulled the drop cloth off the piano and settled onto the bench, then played the flowing notes with her eyes closed. She had played this piece at Juilliard for a recital, and her fingers remembered. Then she rested her hands on the keyboard and smiled. The piano was her happy place. Playing helped her concentrate and deal with stress. She regretted that the piano teachers conference had ended in trauma. She regretted that her memories of Door County would always include this hard story.

Piper even regretted that her fears about glamping had come true. Rosie loved Bess the glamper, but Piper would never go glamping again.

A knock at the door interrupted her thoughts, and she yelled, "Come in, Rosie!" She turned and her cheeks reddened. "Oh, Chief Maxwell, I'm sorry. I would have opened the door instead of hollering if I knew you were at the door."

He smiled. "No problem, Miss Haydn. Lovely music. You chose the right career."

"Thank you. What can I do for you?"

"Can we sit?"

"Yes, but follow me in here. My wallpaper project got derailed by Rosie's injury, and my turret is a mess."

He raised an eyebrow and winked.

Piper swallowed and cleared her throat. His wink stirred the butterflies in her stomach and her cheeks warmed. "In here."

He followed her and settled on the sofa. "I have an update from the Department of Justice on the Sharpes. But first I wanted to thank you for going glamping with Rosie. I collected quite a jackpot on my bet."

Piper rolled her eyes. "Go ahead with the update. I'm ignoring your other comment."

He smiled and cleared his throat. "As you know, Clifford died at the scene. The investigation corroborates Rosie's story. Carl shot him as they argued over the split of the jewel." He glanced at her over the top of his notebook.

"Go ahead," Piper said.

"The Sharpes did not recover the diamond; however, the county and the museum funded a dig and found the buried box. They safely tucked the diamond away until the museum can either install stronger safety measures or host an auction."

"Sell it? That's sad."

"Selling the jewel will fund the museum for many decades."

"Good point. What else?"

Chief Maxwell flipped a page in the notebook and tapped his pen on the paper. "Carl and Sheriff Marks are waiting for their trial. I'm assuming the charges will involve murder, kidnapping, and attempted murder, for starters."

"Will we have to testify?"

"They will notify you when the trial date gets closer."

"What about C#?"

"You knew her previously?"

"Yes, since we were kids. She attended school here for a couple of years, but we didn't get along."

"She took part in the scheme enough to face some legal trouble, but she didn't shoot anyone and she's cooperating with authorities. She's out of jail, but the other two remain incarcerated until their court date."

"That's it?"

"I believe so," Chief Maxwell said.

"Thank you for the update. I wanted to thank you for taking care of me that night. I appreciated having you there. I fell apart."

He smiled. "I'm glad I helped you carry that burden."

"Oh, how much do I owe you for the clothes you bought me? The scarf is perfect, by the way. Exactly my style."

He waved a hand. "No, I don't need anything."

Piper scowled. "Chief Maxwell, you don't earn much money in this little town, and the shop in Door County probably charged you a premium for that outfit."

"I was happy to help. No need to repay me," he said. "But I have been wondering if you'd like to go to dinner with me sometime."

Piper cleared her throat. "Did you say dinner?"

"Yes." He smiled and raised an eyebrow. "If you don't mind being seen in public with me, that is."

Piper's chin raised, and she nodded. "You'll have to take me somewhere out of town. Everyone will talk if you take me to a restaurant in Cranberry Harbor."

"What about Sweetberry's?" he asked with a grin.

Piper laughed. "Oh, man—Dominique would call my parents before we ordered the meal."

"Out of town then, Miss Haydn." He nodded and turned to leave.

"Is this a date, Chief Maxwell?" Piper blushed, and the butterflies stampeded in her stomach.

"I do believe so, Miss Haydn," he said and winked before he disappeared.

Rosie popped open Piper's front door. "Hullloooo!" she yelled in a singsong voice.

"In the turret, Rosie."

Rosie plopped onto the sofa in the middle of the room. "Man, who's your interior designer? This place is a wreck." She giggled, her tinkly laugh filling the room.

Piper threw a pillow at Rosie. "Her name is Roosevelt, and she's seriously slacking on her end of the bargain. I might fire her."

Rosie laughed again and tossed the pillow back. "I hope to feel up to it soon. I'm sorry I left it like this before the conference."

"I'll survive. Where did you get that outfit? Wait—don't tell me. The Cranberry Closet?"

"Yep. I found it right before . . . well, before all the commotion." She stood and twirled. Her red curls bounced and the bright purple and blue of the shift dress spun color like a kaleidoscope. Rosie tapped the pointed white polyester collar. "Isn't this amazing? It's the biggest collar I've ever found."

Piper rolled her eyes. "Your dress is a perfect Rosie dress. Where are your go-go boots?"

Rosie squealed. "Oh, friend—you gave me my next thrift store goal!" She plopped down on the sofa and fluffed her curls. "So why was Officer Hunky here?"

"Good grief, Rosie. When will you stop saying that?"

Rosie laughed. "When he's no longer hunky."

"He updated me about C# and her brothers. He also said that the museum might sell the Duchess' diamond to fund their programs."

"Not a bad idea," Rosie said. "But I hope they'll display the diamond for a while. I want to see the rock in person since I got shot over it and everything."

Piper smoothed the fabric on the pillow. "How are you feeling?"

"Better every day. Enough about me. If Officer Hunky only came to update you, why did I see so much pink in your cheeks when I arrived?" She waggled her eyebrows at Piper and giggled when Piper's cheeks blushed again.

"He asked me out for dinner," Piper whispered.

Rosie shrieked and jumped up and down. She ran to Piper and squeezed her. "Yes! He liiiiiiikes you!" Rosie made a heart with her fingers and winked at Piper.

"He bought an outfit for me in Door County because I needed to change out of my evening dress to search for you. I never paid him back, so he said if I let him take me to dinner, he'd consider the bill settled."

"Sure. That's all," Rosie said. "My brothers drove up to retrieve Bess today. I hope she's no worse for the wear. We can try another trip in the spring." She smiled at Piper with an innocent grin.

"Oh, no, Roosevelt Hale. Not me. You'll find someone who enjoys all that fresh air and the pine trees, but I'm never glamping again."

"You said that before. I'll convince you one of these days. All of that mess isn't Bess's fault. She's probably up there crying her eyes out that you don't like her."

"Rosie, campers don't cry."

"Mine does. And she's a glamper if you remember correctly," Rosie said and burst into laughter. She rubbed the fabric on the sofa cushion and bit her lip. "Feels good to laugh, you know?" A tear glistened in her eye.

Piper stood from the floor and joined Rosie on the sofa, pulling her into a gentle hug so she wouldn't hurt her injury. "I'm sorry—for everything. We got caught in a messy family situation and they ruined your debut camping trip. You're right—it's not Bess's fault." She patted Rosie and sniffed the air. "Was that dress stored in mothballs or something? Goodness, Rosie." She moved back to the floor and stacked her music.

"You picked a composer for the spring recital?"

"Rachmaninoff for the seniors." She pointed to the stack of music. "Are you able to come back to work soon?"

"Doctor said another week or two. I'll be good as new."

Piper smiled. "Good—your little students miss you." A knock interrupted her, and Rosie hurried to answer the door.

Dominique waited, holding several to-go boxes. She pushed past Rosie and took the food to the kitchen. "Come, my loves. Dominique needs to put some meat on those bones."

Rosie and Piper followed her and settled at Piper's counter. Dominique unpacked boxes and pulled plates from the cupboard.

"I made you two weaklings another batch of po'boys with less heat for the Wisconsin palate." She smiled and adjusted her apron. "Sit. I need your opinion."

Piper and Rosie reached for the sandwiches and dug in. "Mmm . . ." Rosie said with a mouth full of sandwich. "Delicious. You are a treasure, Miss Dominique."

Dominique smiled and waved a finger at Rosie. "The next time you scare us like that, Rosie, I'm going to . . . well, I don't know what I'm going to do, but I didn't like it one bit."

Rosie jumped from the stool and hurried to Dominique's side. Dominique wrapped her slim brown arms around Rosie and pulled her close. "My babies don't need any ugliness. I can't even think about what we would have done if something had happened to you." She wiped her eyes.

"Nothing happened to me, Miss Dominique." She held the sandwich in the air. "And I'm here to taste this pile of deliciousness."

Dominique laughed. "Girl, don't tell Robby I was over here crying like a fool." She wiped her hands on one of Piper's towels. "I need to get back to Sweetberry's. I wanted to see for myself that you two girls are fine."

"We are," Piper said. "Thank you, Miss Dominique."

Dominique blew a kiss to the girls. "You sit. I'll see myself out. You baby girls take it easy. You promise?"

"Yes, ma'am," Rosie and Piper said and waved to Dominique as she closed the front door.

Rosie licked her fingers. "Oh, I almost forgot." She reached into the pocket of her vintage dress and held out a paper. "Mr. Standerwick is hiring a housekeeper. I might apply."

Piper raised an eyebrow. "Fergus? Why would you want to work for Fergus?"

Rosie laughed. "Might be interesting. Can you imagine seeing the inside of that mansion?"

"Can you imagine dealing with his crankiness all day? I don't have the energy for that."

"What if I can talk him into decorating for Christmas?" Her eyes sparkled. "That enormous mansion all decked out with lights and wreaths."

"I can't remember that house ever having Christmas decorations."

"What about when Mrs. Standerwick was alive? What happened to her anyway?"

"I don't know. That was long before my time."

"I'm going to apply and see what happens," Rosie said. "Can't hurt anything, and the interview is at the mansion, so I can take a peek even if they don't hire me."

"You are a brave, adventurous soul, my friend."

"Either that or stupid." Rosie stuck her tongue out and crossed her eyes.

Piper laughed. "You're not stupid, Rosie. You're a fabulous, creative friend, and you keep me from sinking into spinsterhood."

"Oh, I'm pretty sure Mr. Hunky Police Chief plans to keep you from sinking into spinsterhood." She squealed when Piper threw a tomato slice at her.

"That's it," Piper said. "Time for you to get out of here and let me have some peace. I have an academy to run and students to teach. No time for foolishness." She winked at Rosie.

"I'll go, but I'm not taking back what I said about Mr. Hunky." Rosie stuck out her tongue and skipped down Piper's hall. She stood at the door and called, "Arrivederci, my darling."

Piper followed her and leaned on the doorjamb and watched Rosie back out of the driveway. She waved until her friend's car drove out of sight.

She shut the door and picked up the piles of music spread across the turret floor. She propped a piece of music on the ledge of her grand piano and sat down to play, breathing a prayer of thankfulness for Rosie's safety and healing and that their lives would soon settle back into the quiet, charming life she loved so much—a life where nothing more exciting happened than choosing between Sweetberry's or Ruby's and where her life revolved around music, coffee, and her students.

She smiled a lopsided grin as she played. "I cannot believe you talked me into going glamping, Roosevelt Hale. Never again," she whispered as her fingers moved across the keys. She glanced out the window and let out the breath she had held since the night Rosie went missing. "Thank you, Lord, for my home, and thank you for Cranberry Harbor, USA."

Her brand new beautiful grand piano has just one problem. It came with a bonus corpse and now she's at the top of the suspect list.

If you'd like to find out what happened in Piper and Rosie's first adventure, check out Murder Goes Solo.

Sign up for my email list to receive a set of Rosie paper dolls.

Murder Goes Glamping
Play List

Chopin: Nocturne Op 9 No 1 in B flat minor

Rachmaninoff: The Isle of the Dead
Rachmaninoff: Opus 21 No. 7
Rachmaninoff: Piano Concerto No. 2

Shostakovich: Piano Concerto No. 1
Shostakovich: Waltz No. 2
Shostakovich: Concerto No. 2
Shostakovich: The Gadfly Suite, Opus 97a

Tangled Lines: Back Home
Tchaikovsky: Swan Lake

ACKNOWLEDGEMENTS

A thank you to —

M. Brian Smith, communications supervisor, Winnebago County Sheriff's Office, Oshkosh, Wisconsin, for 9-1-1 protocol and wording.

Chief Aaron Chapin for answering police procedural questions.

*My siblings, *Rebekah Kotlar, Rachel Hershberger, and John Bonner*. What would I do without you? From my first rambling thoughts to the finished product, you give me ideas, critiques, and encouragement. Love you.

J. Dahlke RN, BSN, CNI, for helping me understand what a body shot and left for dead may look like.

Alissa Schwalbach, my Door County, Wisconsin, expert. Thanks for making sure my details are correct. And thanks for owning Beach Road Cottage. We love spending time there.

The Drone Lady, AKA Rachael Dowling for sharing drone information and Wisconsin drone laws with me.

*My alpha team: *Karla Bolender, John Bonner, Laurie Herlich, Rachel Hershberger, Jackie Koll, Rebekah Kotlar, Marsha Landro, Christina Lyon, Jenna McGlone, Miranda Pautz, Shelly Smith, Crystal Thornton, Tricia Troyer, Kristi Welch Van Zanten*. Thank you for making me work hard to write a great story. I appreciate all your help, encouragement, and mistake-finding.

You. Thank you for joining me for another Piper Haydn adventure. Please remember to leave a review and recommend my book to your friends.

Afterword

I enjoyed sending Piper and Rosie to Door County in *Murder Goes Glamping.* Door County, Wisconsin, is the peninsula jutting out into Lake Michigan and it is beautiful year-round. Door County is one of my favorite places to visit. I'm with Rosie on this one—I would love to own a vintage glamper and glamp in Door County in comfort and style.

Beach Road Cottage is an actual Airbnb in Sister Bay, Wisconsin. A dear friend of mine owns the cottage on the land her great-grandfather farmed when he emigrated from Sweden. We love staying there and you will too. As an added bonus, she and her husband donate a portion of their proceeds to Flying Free to support women fleeing domestic violence.

When you visit Door County you can drive through Peninsula State Park and see the Eagle Tower. You can explore Horseshoe Island—yes, a wealthy family owned it and built their summer retreat on the island, and some evidence of that is still visible on the island. You can eat at a restaurant with goats on the roof, weather permitting. If you do that, make sure you try the lingonberries. Enjoy a sunset over the water, stop for ice cream at the red-and-white ice cream shop, and drive down the winding road near Gills Rock.

About this diamond heist . . . gotcha! Too unbelievable to be real, right? Well, I made it up, but it's true nevertheless. Let me explain. A man digging a well in Eagle, Wisconsin, found a large stone in 1876. Tiffany's purchased the 16.25-carat diamond, then JP Morgan purchased the stone to display in the American Museum of Natural History. The Eagle Diamond remained in an exhibit in the museum for sixty-five years before a thief named "Murph the Smurf" stole the gem—can you believe that? What a name! The Eagle Diamond remains lost. Who knows? What if Murph the Smurf hid the jewel in Peninsula State Park? I don't condone digging up campsites, so don't get me in trouble by making a mess around the park when you look for the diamond. Read about the Eagle Diamond.

But the Wallis Simpson stuff? Come on—who did I think I would fool? I'm a fiction author, after all, and I must balance writing a fun story with keeping it believable, so while I make up many elements of my story, I don't want to stretch believability too far. How many times did you roll your eyes when I said that Wallis Simpson vacationed in Door County? Tell the truth.

Guess what? It's true. Wallis Warfield vacationed in Door County, Wisconsin, with the family of her fiancé, Earl Winfield Spencer Jr., and they spent their newlywed summer at the family's vacation home. She befriended Lizzie Anderson from Ephraim, Wisconsin—one of the small towns in Door County—and invited her to her first wedding. Read all about it here and check out these photos.

Mrs. John Freeman Rasin

requests the honour of your presence

at the marriage of her daughter

Wallis Warfield

to

E. Winfield Spencer, junior

Lieutenant United States Navy

on Wednesday evening, the eighth of November

at half after six o'clock

Christ Church

Baltimore, Maryland

Images courtesy of the Ephraim Historical Society, Ephraim,
Wisconsin

Thank you for reading my book. I hope you enjoyed Piper and
Rosie's second adventure. Please sign up for my email list and
receive a free set of Rosie paper dolls.

Malissa Chapin

MEET THE AUTHOR

Malissa Chapin has a heart for writing stories filled with humor, faith, and truth. She's always adored reading excellent books and is tickled to see her childhood dream of becoming an author finally come true.

Malissa loves creating with words, watercolor, fabric, and yarn. You can find her in her garden, at the piano, homeschooling her bonus baby, or enjoying a coffee with friends.

She lives and sometimes freezes in Wisconsin with her family and a crazy cat.

Sign up for her newsletter at www.malissachapin.com and be the first to hear about her works in progress, offers, and fun news.